Tomy and the Planet of Lies

By

Erich von Däniken

Translated by Nicholas Quaintmere

Tantor
m e d i a

Tantor Media, Inc.
2 Business Park Road
Old Saybrook, CT 06475

www.tantor.com

Tomy and the Planet of Lies

ISBN: 9780988349438

Printed in the United States of America

First Tantor Media printing, October 2012

THE DECISION

His very existence was an impossibility. An anachronism. Looking at it from a scientific point of view, Tomy shouldn't have existed at all, and yet he had been there—utterly real, and with a human body. Regardless of what science had to say about it. At any rate, Tomy was here and lived among us for several weeks and that was enough time for him to get to know plenty of people, both good and bad. God knows I wasn't the only one that knew Tomy. Though I have to say that only a handful of people knew what I knew, and those who didn't belong to this inner circle really had no idea who Tomy actually was.

Sometimes, in secluded moments, holding a glass of red wine up in front of my eyes, I was overcome by a great fear that I had dreamt the whole episode with Tomy. But Tomy wasn't a ghost. At home absolutely everything reminded me of him: his room, the furniture, even the knives and forks. When signals like that are flying at you from every direction, you can't really escape your past. So I tried to find an excuse and pain-fully realized that Tomy would have reprimanded me for my lying. As a result, as I said to Mario, the bar-man in the Suvretta House Hotel, I had suddenly felt that a change of air would do me good. And the air in St. Moritz seemed the best air of all.

"A wise decision," said Mario and started telling me about various incidents that he had experienced during his 30 years at the Suvretta House Hotel. As I listened to Mario's accounts I honestly felt my breath catch in my throat.

Seeing as most of the guests at this time of the evening were still chatting away in the dining room, I invited Mario to join me in a bottle of champagne. He declined, as he had only just started his shift.

Three hours later, still propped on my stool and staring bleary-eyed through the array of bottles lining the mirrored wall behind the bar, I thought I saw the examining magistrate from Solothurn coming towards me. "Send that man away," I commanded Mario. But he couldn't see anyone, and his assistant too assured me that no one was there.

It's now around 11 o'clock in the morning and the young ice princesses are turning pirouettes on the ice rink down below. I'm totally embarrassed that I threw my glass at the mirrored wall last night. I apologized profusely to Mario and generously recompensed him for the damage. At least that grinning face had disap-peared after my clattering throw. Later on, I will go and apologize to the hotel director and say to him that I cannot explain my wild outburst and that it must be due to being overworked. And in the very moment that I am concocting up my excuse for my poor behavior, I feel the touch of breath behind me that I had felt so often during those weeks when Tomy had starred over my shoulder while I was working at my desk. I can hear him gently mocking me: "Erich, that lie is totally unnecessary."

Great! But what are you supposed to do when you can't tell the truth because it's too unbelievable?

The hotel director didn't hold my excessive behavior against me, although he let me know, in his extremely distinguished manner, that repeating the event would be severely frowned upon. I took his hand and promised him he had nothing to worry about. And I didn't feel that I was lying.

In the meantime, a few rays of sunshine have begun to poke through the clouds. I'm sitting with a strong cup of black tea in front of me, trying to come to grips with myself and my situation.

It's exactly two days since the examining magistrate from Solothurn revealed that—for the time being—he would not need any more statements from me. For the time being. With these people you never know what's coming later. They had questioned me for days: the experts, the forensic specialists, the detectives and, of course, the dogged examining magistrate. Kellehans, he was called. Killer Hans, more like. They had wanted to know every single tiny detail about what had happened, and—with hindsight—I should be happy that they didn't take me into custody. I told the truth. In every single interview. Nobody believed a word. Not even after Marc, who had been there from the very beginning, had corroborated every single word in separate interrogation, and not even after my wife, Elisabeth, had also confirmed every one of my statements. Even the gentlemen who were grilling me could understand my frustration. And I could understand the questioners, too, because what I had experienced was utterly impossible. A man materializes out of thin air and then, just as suddenly, disappears after spending several weeks living at my side. And every-

3

one had seen him, talked to him, and asked him questions. Who was going to buy that? Even though it was the truth, pure and simple.

The experts had been the worst. They had torn me apart on a daily basis and I had experienced some really bizarre moments. Everyone believed everyone and no one believed anyone. What good were articles of clothing, shoes, a watch, and underwear? What good were fingerprints, when their owner hadn't even been good enough to leave a body behind? A body, by the way, that—even if it had existed—was not of this earth and yet nevertheless was a human being. A body that had no birth certificate, no baptism certificate, no scholastic records, and no earthly past whatsoever, aside from the weeks that he had spent among us.

At any rate, they had confiscated a letter from Tomy—scribbled down in blue ballpoint in his handwriting that looked so infuriatingly similar to my own, which made the whole thing even more complicated. This letter, written to my housekeeper Edith, had provided the police with Tomy's fingerprints. But, impossibly, Tomy had exactly the same fingerprints as me. Something that had never been seen anywhere in the world. Everyone has his own, unique fingerprints. Except for Tomy and me! The examining magistrate had held the fingerprints up under my nose. Tomy's and mine. They were identical.

"So *you* are the corpse!" he screamed at me.

I shouted back, just as loud.

"But you can see that I'm standing in front of you!" I said. "Alive, for God's sake! I've explained to you a thousand times how Tomy came into being. And his fingerprints are the proof: he was a copy of me! Have you never heard of clones?"

The examining magistrate just laughed at that and said spitefully that I didn't need to come up with such nonsense. Human cloning was impossible, not to mention the fact that there had not been nearly enough time. Then he held up Tomy's passport. It was a replacement passport, issued by the Swiss embassy in Teheran.

"And this?" his asked, impatiently, "Is this some kind of ghost? A Swiss passport, made out for an Anton von Däniken, born April 24, 1957, 169 centimeters tall, brown eyes, brown hair, and distinguishing features: a mole on the back of the left hand, although no Anton von Däniken was ever born in Zofingen on April 24, 1957. Do you take us for idiots?"

They would eventually figure what was rotten in the state of Denmark. Moreover, he slyly pointed out, waving his finger threateningly towards me, that if Tomy and I were so identical and now one of us was missing, then I could just as easily be the copy and it was the real Erich von Däniken who had been murdered. "Prove to me," he demanded, slamming his fist into the table, "that you are the original!"

"But you already know from my wife, from Marc and all the other witnesses that Tomy was thirty years younger than me," I moaned back at him. "I'm 52 years old! Or do I look to you like a 22-year-old?"

In the light of all these improbable events, I had spontaneously decided to leave Solothurn and come here. I knew the Suvretta House Hotel in St. Moritz from earlier visits. I had called the examining magistrate beforehand and put him in the picture regarding my new whereabouts—public prosecutors and Swiss examining magistrates are no different; you never knew when they might change their minds and lead them to issue a warrant for your arrest. I was only allowed to go on condition that I called Solothurn once a day. If I didn't call, for whatever reason, the authorities would assume that I was attempting to flee justice.

It was now, while drinking my third cup of Darjeeling tea, that I came up with my plan to write down the events of the previous few weeks. No, not for the benefit of others, but rather so that I could get straight in my own head what had really happened.

True, I had—now and again—taken a close look at myself to see if I had been suffering from hallucinations. To see if I had duped Marc, my wife, and all the others who knew Tomy. Whenever I needed reassurance, I called Marc—or one of the others involved—and asked them to recount certain situations to me, just using key words. But my memory of the events always proved to be perfect. Everyone else's experiences with Tomy were exactly the same as mine.

I wrote down these key words until late in the night. At around two in the morning, I called Marc—dragging him out of sleep—and asked him what Tomy's first words had been. I had written down the words as I remembered them before I had dialed. Marc pleaded for a moment to get his head together. Then he slowly quoted Tomy's first words. They had obviously left a pretty strong impression in his memory, too, because what he now said matched what I had written exactly—word for word. "You don't really want to shoot yourself, do you?" had been the first thing that we had heard from Tomy's lips. I thanked Marc profusely, but warned him that he could look forward to further calls. But for the rest of that night I let him have his peace.

***

I have a wonderful view of the Corvatsch, the famous mountain just south of St. Moritz. The sky is now the kind of blue that you can only see in Engadin. My thoughts are suddenly captivated by the rocky cliffs and glaciers; they lose themselves somewhere where

6

only thoughts can go. If only the piece of paper covered in my scribbled notes wasn't lying there on the table. Suddenly my idea to write everything down seems futile. Who would ever believe any of it anyway? I'm not related to Marc in any way; he was my secretary back then and is my friend now. And during that dangerous trip through the highlands of Pakistan, he had also proved to be an extremely reliable partner. He is much younger than me, and of course I felt responsible for him because I had persuaded him to take this trip. For him, if no one else, I would write down that bizarre sequence of events so that he, too, could finally be rid of his nightmares.

Marc hasn't slept properly since the day he met Tomy. His mother recently told me that Marc had cried out during the night. What he had said, she hadn't been able to understand, but she had found him sitting up in bed, drenched in sweat.

When I hear stories like that I ask myself if we had ever really had a chance to free ourselves of Tomy. It's true that he was a man like us, of flesh and blood, even if he did appear under highly mysterious circumstances. And then he disappeared under even more mysterious circumstances. Of course, we could never have just left him there defenseless and alone in the cold, early dawn. Especially with the knowledge that the rising sun would bring with it temperatures that would mean an agonizing death for anyone left alone in the desert.

And because we didn't leave him there, we ended up living through an adventure that, in the end, left us looking like murderers. Marc and I know that we're not murderers, and my wife knows it too, but we suspect that none of the officers investigating the case are quite so convinced of our innocence. If they were, we might have been able to carry out the perfect murder.

What I now write—from my memory, the notes of the previous night, and several phone conversations with Marc—is basically the story that the examining magistrate Kellerhans already knows. Marc and I had to make countless statements to the effect. But the difference between all those civil servants and us is that, although they didn't believe a word of what we said, we know with absolute certainty that is exactly how it was.

THE DAYBREAK WHEN TOMY
CAME INTO BEING

Quetta, Pakistan. A city of 200,000 souls at the crossing point of the roads from Kandahar, in Afghanistan, Zaidan, in Iran, and Multan and Sukkur, in Pakistan—where we had just come from. This ancient Mogul city is now industrialized and relatively clean, and even has a halfway decent hotel, which—bizarrely enough—is called Lourdes after the city in France where the Virgin Mary appeared to a young girl.

Despite the hotel's Christian-sounding name, which seemed so out of place in a city of Moslems, I had seen no sign of God; otherwise I might have stayed a bit longer in Quetta. The blue plaster that covered the two-story hotel building was peeling off in several places, revealing an older clay wall strengthened with straw and, here and there, the odd stone. The room that Marc and I were sharing had a stuffy smell of old turpentine and insecticide. On the ceiling a decrepit fan turned lazily as if it had been slowly poisoned by years of exposure to so many pesticides.

We had arrived the previous afternoon, following

a roundabout journey from Multan. It was a roundabout journey because the Indus had again broken free of its banks and all the usual routes to Quetta had either been blocked or simply washed away. Our next port of call was to be the Iranian border town of Zahedan, which was 721 kilometers distant from Quetta, across the Baluchistan desert.

Baluchistan, which contains the districts of Quetta and historic Kalat, covers an area of nearly 350,000 square kilometers and, at that time, was home to approximately 4 million people. Of these a considerable amount are nomads, who regularly wander across the borders to Iran and Afghanistan with their herds of sheep. There are strong political groups here who would like to see the region win its independence from Pakistan. These ambitions are given emphasis by the many bandits who break out from their mountain hideouts to attack military convoys or to rob travelers.

We had been warned not to travel across this part of Baluchistan without a military escort. The previous evening we had been told we should make contact with the brigadier of Quetta district responsible for such matters, and—after some telephoning around—we eventually organized a meeting with him before dinner in his office in the military headquarters.

"How many people are in your party? Which vehicle will you be using? What color is it? Have you got any weapons? Do you have a radio?"

He wanted to know the answers to these and many more questions. And early this morning he had called us at the Hotel Lourdes.

"You can travel without an escort!" he said. "We have the route under control. All of our posts have been informed about your beige Range Rover. Stay in your vehicle if people in plain clothes attempt to stop you. If worst comes to worst, just put your foot down and drive away as quickly as possible behind the nearest rock outcropping and then zigzag your way out of there. Make sure you raise plenty of dust: that'll mean they won't be able to see you. Your car is much quicker than the clapped- out old vehicles they'll be driving anyway. Good luck!"

The night before, Marc and I had been up till ten o'clock packing the car. Boxes filled with 2-liter bottles of mineral water, a spare jerry can of petrol, an additional 100 liters of water in four large canisters, and a plastic bottle of distilled water for the batteries in case they dried out. On top of this we placed the toolbox, spare wheels, maps, and compass, taking care not to forget the pistol and tear gas spray—hidden away but easy to get to. And, of course, we packed the camera cases and so on. After we'd finished our work, the hotel owner kindly let us use his kitchen to cook up some spaghetti and tomato sauce. We served it up with a bottle of red wine, which was light enough that we wouldn't have too much trouble getting up the next morning.

At six thirty a.m. we were ready to set off. The concierge of the Lourdes, a refined old Englishman who'd been in the country for years, slammed the rear doors of the car shut and then stood there and waved, shouting out: "Good luck!"

I started up the motor and scoffed: "Well, Marc, let's be going then! May Saint Christopher watch over us!"

"I don't know him. What does he do then?" asked Marc.

"Heavens above, lad! Where were you when you were supposed to be in religious instruction? Saint Christopher is one of the Fourteen Holy Helpers. He is the patron saint of sailors and waggoners…and, hopefully, of people crossing deserts."

Marc crossed himself, rather clumsily, as he's not even catholic. "May Saint Christopher forgive me!" But the saint must have been put out by Marc's ignorance, as events were about to show.

After only half an hour on the road, we were already in the mountains. Not mountains like I know them from Switzerland, however. Here there were no plants or snow, no green blades of grass or mountain streams—only the railway track which runs from Sukkur to Zahedan. We saw three stations, but not a single train.

Every half hour we were stopped by military patrols. Officers checked our passports and after a few minutes' palaver allowed us to continue on our way with an ironic "Good luck!" For about 60 kilometers, our route was accompanied by a telephone cable running along at ground level next to the road. It was comforting to know that we were somehow still connected to civilization. We were making good progress and by midday we had already covered a third of our journey when we were suddenly confronted by a roadblock constructed from large blocks of stone, which had been laid haphazardly across the road. Behind them stood one man in uniform accompanied by four others in civilian clothing, their machine pistols casually pointed at the floor.

The uniformed man ordered me to get out of the car, which was exactly what the brigadier had warned me not to do. Why were the other men not in uniforms? Were they no longer part of the Pakistani Army? The uniformed man pointed at the metal cases on the rear seat of the car. I knew that there were ignorant people around who liked opening up technical equipment, or pulling out the contents of exposed film rolls only then to exclaim that the films have nothing on them. My aluminum cases housed metal detectors, which were sensitive instruments, easily damaged by careless handling.

Suddenly, I had a bright idea. I smiled my best smile and reached deliberately with my right hand for the console in the middle of the car. My Polaroid camera was lying there. I slowly pointed it at Marc and pressed the button; then I aimed the lens at the uniformed man and smiled even more sweetly than before. Right after I pressed the button, the Polaroid picture whirred out of the camera's slit. Still smiling in an affable manner, I tore off the protective strip from the picture and waved it around, fanning myself in the process. When the uniformed man saw his own likeness appearing in full color about a minute later, he must have thought I was some kind of magician.

The turban-wearing civilians laid their machine pistols on the floor and gawped over their boss's shoulder. Then they all wanted just such a picture for themselves and then finally a group picture with me. Marc shot the 'family portrait' from the car window and passed me the camera. I asked him to hand me a new packet of film—it was the last Polaroid film we had. Laughing I asked the five men to sit on the stones blocking the road and took two more pictures.

After this display of magic, I began to heave one of the stones off the road and gestured to the men to help me with the others. After I gave the camera to the officer and showed him how to press the button, the others joined in with my stone-clearing activities. I got back behind the wheel and we waved and laughed, and then I put my foot down. It was the last checkpoint we came across and to this day, I don't know whether it was a genuine one or not, or how long it had taken those road-blockers to realize that after the film had run out there would be no more magic pictures sliding out of the camera slit.

The mountains lay behind us, and ahead of us stretched the endless desert, initially flanked on the right by the foothills, which gradually faded away as we drove on. The road became more of a dirt track, the surface transforming into a kind of corrugated strip with furrows spaced around 15 to 20 centimeters apart.

Initially, I tried driving slowly over them but the Range Rover clattered, shook, and vibrated unbearably. Finally, I figured out that a driving speed of about 60 to 70 kilometers per hour was ideal. The only danger at that speed was where sudden sand drifts covered the bumpy road. If the wheels were caught at an angle in the sand the car would skid around in an instant—like on black ice, but without ice's advantages: that you could see it and that it stopped at the edge of the road. Here, on the other hand, lurked quicksand where the whole vehicle could sink into the sand without leaving a trace.

Sitting behind the wheel, I felt like one of those bulky men operating a jackhammer. Every bump was transmitted along my arms to my elbows. How long would the car hold out? The grey-beige color of the Range Rover was slowly being completely blanked out by white sand dust. How long would the air filter cope with that? When would the spark plugs and the distributor give up the ghost? Please, holy Saint Christopher, anything but a breakdown in this awful heat. The external temperature was now at about 50 degrees Celsius; I couldn't lean my elbows out of the open window anymore because the metal of the doors was now hot enough to fry bacon.

At around four in the afternoon, we saw a few houses in the middle of this forsaken desert. I drove up towards them until we could see a signboard bearing the legend: Customs. What was all that about? A customs post here in the middle of the desert? A lonely, old soldier in a dark brown t-shirt explained that this was the last Pakistani settlement, 200 kilometers before the Iranian border. He demanded twenty dollars in small bills, which I paid and then asked what the people here actually did. "Nothing," he said. "We're just here to keep an eye on the boarder." The name of this desert backwater was Nok Kundi.

We had just driven across purgatory and now we were driving directly into hell itself. The desert track became even more irregular, the gaps between the furrows in the road were randomly spaced, and the sudden sand drifts more frequent. There may have been no water here as far as the eye could see, but at least once a year it must rain cats and dogs because every once in a while the track simply disappeared, as if washed away. It wasn't possible to manage much more than jogging tempo, no more than 20 kilometers per hour. In the rearview mirror I could see our endless dust trail rising up into the twilight, fanning out behind us like a pale gray veil.

Seven p.m. The heat was still oppressive. Position: still 126 kilometers to the Iranian border in the desert of Baluchistan. Throughout the whole day, we had not seen a single vehicle apart from ourselves on the road.

Marc's face was swollen, his eyes rimmed with red. Sweat was pouring out of every pore, but despite the heat, he was shivering. It was clear that he had some kind of fever: he coughed and wheezed like someone with some kind of lung disease. I vaguely recalled something about dust allergies so I moistened a cloth with mineral water and wrapped it around his mouth and nose. I drove on with Marc sitting next to me wrapped up like a mummy, occasionally gasping and coughing, but it was hard work. One kilometer after the next. The massive, blazing gold disc of the sun sank slowly down behind a massive sand dune and suddenly the heat relented. Our position was now 98 kilometers from the Iranian border. Marc's condition still had me worried, however. We decided to call it a day. We would spend the night here and give Marc's immune system a bit of a chance to regenerate. It would have been foolish to try to carry on anyway. The sand drifts don't show up well in the headlights.

This was the incredible night when Tomy came into being. Marc and I will never be able to forget the events of that night. It all began with Marc's chattering teeth and from a fever. He got himself some medication to reduce fever and some antihistamines from our onboard first aid kit and washed them down with generous amounts of mineral water. To give him enough room to lie down properly across the front seats of the car, I made myself a bed on the roof, the rear seats being packed full with our equipment.

Occasionally a cool desert breeze wafted through the night, blowing fine dust into my eyes, ears, nose, and mouth, penetrating the warmth of my woolen blanket. I looked up at the starry skies above me, the way they only appear in the middle of a desert. Clearer and brighter than any planetarium, those strange, heavenly bodies seemed so close that I could simply reach out and grab them. Despite being numb with fatigue, I stayed awake. Below me, Marc still coughed. Every movement he made was amplified by the car's suspension across the chassis. Sometime after midnight, I finally dozed off, but woke again around an hour later shivering with the cold.

I stared at the glittering jewels of the night sky and began to daydream. Somewhere out there, in the endless expanse of space, spaceships would be zooming around from planet to planet, bringing post and strange wares from bizarre worlds to distant outposts of the Milky Way, perhaps there would even be wars between planets or solar systems. Maybe even now information was flashing between the constellation of Pleiades and the planets of Polaris, our North Star. We human beings, we microscopic mites down below, don't have the slightest inkling of it all. Never had I seen the constellation of Lyra so clearly as in this night. I knew that its main star, Vega, was fifty times brighter than our sun, but on this night, for the very first time, I could clearly make out its blue coloration with the naked eye.

I wondered how many planets might be in orbit around Vega. I recalled that Lyra was famous for its double-double star, an absolute rarity in our galaxy. Astronomers believe that the possibility of life in a double star system is very slight, if not non-existent, as the constant radiation from the binary suns would make the emergence of life impossible. But what makes them so sure about it? Maybe life forms have evolved under quite conditions than we can imagine. Maybe... maybe... maybe there are solar systems with binary stars populated by gaseous intelligent beings, maybe they don't even need space ships to travel the unimaginable distances between the stars. Maybe there is so much that is so completely different to what we assume. I would give my life to be able to fly out into the universe, past the glowing suns, violet planets and—why not?—life forms that look like giant spiders. Although I cannot, for the life of me, stand the creatures normally.

I felt like a microbe stranded on a crumb of bread, and although I was free to hop around the place as much as I liked, I would never make it out of the bakery. I had heard plenty of UFO stories, but I had never seen a UFO myself. However, tonight, this was what my heart was yearning for. I stared at Vega, with its blue rays, and really began to wish that some being from out there in space would come and visit me. "Come down here! I want to talk to you!" I thought, "Show yourselves, if you're out there!"

Suddenly I recalled the Volga Song from the operetta *The Czarevich*, and began quietly humming to myself:

A soldier stands on the Volga's banks
Standing guarding his fatherland

... and then the refrain:

Have You up there forgotten me too?
My heart is yearning for love so true.
So many angels in heaven abide by Thee,
Send just one of them down here to me.

All kinds of crazy thoughts occurred to me then. "Halloooo, you strangers!" I giggled to myself, "Show yourselves, if you're really there!"

At some stage, I must have nodded off to sleep again for I was suddenly awakened by a flash like lightning.

I started as if a bomb had gone off under me. All around, as far as the eye could see there was no sign of a storm. Then I suddenly had a feeling as if heat was spreading out under the surface of my skull and the moisture between the folds of my grey matter was beginning to bubble and boil. I pressed my hands desperately to my temples and began to shake my head frantically. It seemed to help: the pressure slowly eased. With dawning horror, I recalled reading something about strokes. Had I just had a stroke? Was I going to be partially paralyzed, never be able to speak again? I opened my eyes and saw a dark red band across the horizon—the morning twilight. A second later I heard a shot ring out under me. It sounded like a dry "plop" and Marc started to cry out. The Range Rover started to vibrate violently. I leapt down from the roof and yanked open the driver's door. Had Marc somehow gotten hold of the gun and fired it under his blanket? Was he suffering some kind of delirium, no longer knowing what he was doing? If only I had taken the pistol with me up onto the roof!

"Marc! What are you doing! Wake up! Give me the gun!" I screamed at him, realizing at the same time that my fears about walking and talking were unfounded.

As I had opened the door, the light had automatically come on. Marc stared out at me wide-eyed and said, in a shaky voice:

"I didn't shoot, Erich. The banging is coming from somewhere here in the car."

I went to the rear of the car and fumbled nervously with the lock to the rear door. I swung it upwards and immediately noticed that the window was shattered. I didn't even have time to come up with a theory as to how it could have broken as there was another loud bang, and then a torrent of water, almost like from out of a shower head, hit me right in the face. God damn! I shook my head and went to dry my face on my right sleeve, but my face was completely dry! Not a drop of water, simply nothing.

"Erich!" Marc was clearly having trouble speaking. "Look over there!"

He was pointing at something on the ground, about three meters away from the left-hand side of the car.

There was another bang and I watched as one of the 2-liter water bottles exploded inside the car. The water didn't flood out; didn't create a puddle, but instead, before my very eyes, formed itself into a water funnel, swirling around itself above the exact same spot that Marc was anxiously staring at. It was as if some hidden underground vacuum cleaner was trying to suck it up.

"Marc! Get out of the car!" I screamed, without even really realizing why I said it.

Marc grabbed onto the steering wheel, swung his legs and made his way toward the front of the vehicle. It struck me that he had bare feet and I was thinking to myself, "I hope he doesn't tread on a scorpion," when the next bang cracked through the night, immediately followed by another.

I ran away from the car to what seemed a safe distance, about five meters. Marc ran over to me and we stared goggle- eyed at the events that were playing out before our very eyes above the desert sand. The water from the exploded bottles was swirling through the air to that eerie spot where it coalesced into a floating water funnel. Suddenly there were three more explosions and the water that was released formed another funnel, which then combined with the first floating funnel. A fine mist of water vapor formed and the sand started to move. I thought of one of the larger scorpions digging itself out of the sand, and then some kind of worm. Then it looked more like a small, constantly twitching snake, growing rapidly. The 'snake' seemed to split into several then laced themselves together, a fourth of them forming a kind of translucent head with two large eyes.

We heard another bang—by now around ten of the two-liter bottles must have exploded—and a bent body grew out of the head in front of us.

"It looks like an embryo," said Marc in awe, and I could see that he was right, although my common sense was telling me that I shouldn't believe the evidence of my own eyes. One explosion followed the next inside the car until every single one of the water bottles—it must have been 54 liters of water in all—had burst and the embryo in the desert sand had slowly began to bubble and steam, part of the paint on the car's bodywork started to melt and for a moment I thought I could smell magnesium. (I knew the smell from my schooldays, because we had always rubbed magnesium powder on our hands before doing gymnastics on the horizontal bars). Then there was suddenly a smell of gasoline in the air.

The next thing we heard was some kind of sucking noise, which became a roaring and then a bubbling sound. As if thrown by a ghostly hand, one of our spanners flew through the shattered rear window. Not floating slowly, but at a speed that would have done serious damage to our skulls if we had had the misfortune to be in the way. The water funnel over the sand had disappeared. Where it had been a moment before, the spanner now floated and, I don't how else I could describe it, seemed to be melting in certain places.

Marc and I were horrified. This was definitely no kind of earthly phenomenon—we were witnesses to something uncanny.

Coincidentally, I had written a book some years before about unexplained apparitions and so I was aware of various different types and forms of appearances from the literature.

Now, as I stared dumbfounded at that spot in the sand where the body was forming, I was struck by the similarities to the statements of the Lourdes and Fátima children. Their visions were always heralded by lightning and then followed by electrical discharges, which in turn were associated with rushing, crackling sounds. One of the Fátima children, little Lucia, had stated that before every single appearance she had noticed a noise like a firework rocket exploding in the distance.

All this occurred to me while I—incapable of uttering a single sound—was staring at the apparition slowly taking shape in front of me.

Marc wheezed next to me, "In the name of God, what is it?"

"It must be some kind of vision," I said. "You know, like those ones in Fátima in Portugal. Some kind of strange energy form is materializing here. I remember the statements made by the Fátima children in the transcripts. They said that at first they had seen something that looked like a sack of flour shrouded in a floating veil. I don't think we have too much to fear. That thing will disappear into thin air in a second."

I sounded a lot braver than I actually felt, but I wanted to reassure Marc. My insides, however, were in complete chaos. I was really scared; my heart was pounding so loud I was sure Marc could hear it; and the veins on my temples felt as though they were about to burst. Then I unexpectedly had the feeling that I wasn't alone in my skull. As if I was suddenly schizophrenic, as if all my higher functions were being switched off against my will. Incomprehensibly and quickly, I was overcome by a feeling of leaden tiredness, my knees sagged, and I fell to the ground. The whole thing must have lasted only a few seconds, since Marc grabbed me and cried: "Come on! We've gotta get out of here!"

While I was pulling myself together, a young boy was growing at an alarming pace out of the desert sand in front of us. The boy became a youth with hair on his head and in the pubic regions.

Then there was silence.

Marc and I watched as his chest began to rise and then sink. He breathed deeply and, as it seemed to me, very slowly. His eyes were closed, his hair and body covered in sand. Then the unfathomable creature balled his hands into fists, moved his fingers, his toes, pulled his knees in, stretched his arms out in front of his chest and opened his eyes.

Now I really was thinking about hallucinations. The shock of the last few minutes was not something I could shake off too quickly; the inexplicable exploding water bottles and the flying spanner must have addled my senses. Obviously, I was seeing things that couldn't possibly have happened, like some kind of post-hypnotic suggestion. A suggestion just to clear up the matter is something that influences process of thought, feeling or will, leading to an unconsidered assumption of values. This was what flew through my mind, but it quickly became clear to me that this was no kind of suggestion.

"Marc, what do you see?" I pressed.

I could hear Marc's breathing. He breathed in deeply through his nose and puffed out all of the used up air through his mouth, the way we did when we were hung over and were trying to get as much oxygen as possible into our bodies. Then he gathered his senses together and spoke with almost exaggerated clarity.

"It's a man," he said. "A *naked* man."

That's what I saw, too. The rising sun was now throwing out enough light that we could clearly recognize the young, male body. The face of the stranger seemed to be wearing a smile. All around was utter silence. We stared at each other: Marc and I on the one side, the stranger standing just a few meters away from us.

Alongside us the Range Rover with its shattered rear window and lying in front of us on the floor, directly in front of the stranger's right hand, a spanner, which looked to me to be strangely porous and bent. And there was still the smell of gasoline in the air.

"A monster," said Marc in a calm voice and then

ran the few steps to the car and pulled the gun out from its hiding place. Before he could cock the trigger, I shouted, "No Marc! Don't shoot! Give me the gun!"

I took the safety off and made sure the first round was loaded into the chamber. I had done it so many times during my national service I could do it in my sleep now. No need to look at the gun at all.

Even during the strange process of "creation," I had already noticed that the stranger in the sand looked a hell of a lot like me. However, it was how I had looked thirty years ago, not now. Marc wasn't even born then and he couldn't possibly know how I would have looked as a 22-year-old—after all, I was now 52. Now, as the impossible being squatted in front of us on the floor and stared up at us, it was clear to me: this was a rejuvenated copy of me!

Then the stranger began to smile and my breath almost caught in my throat. In my youth, I had had two prominent, white teeth on my upper jaw, which I had later lost in a car accident. The being on the desert floor had my old teeth! He continued smiling, looked me up and down, and then noticed the gun in my hand.

"You don't really want to shoot yourself, do you?" he said in the voice of my younger days, and what's more in Swiss German! "Yourself" he had said, not "me." Those were his first words, which Marc and I would always both remember exactly.

"Shoot, for God's sake!" shouted Marc, "This monster isn't real!"

The stranger sat down in a crouch, propping himself up on his arms.

"I'm cold," he said, and leaned his head a little to one side, a typical gesture of mine.

"Who are you?" I asked fearlessly, ready at any second to squeeze the trigger.

"I haven't got any name yet. And as to who I

am… you should be able to see that. For goodness sake, it's damn cold here. Erich, help me—please!"

He knew my name! Marc stood next to me and said, flabbergasted:

"It's unbelievable. He speaks Swiss German and knows your name! Have you got an explanation *for this*?"

I didn't. I wandered over to the Range Rover, grabbed Marc's woolen blanket from the front seat and threw it over to the stranger. He stood up, shook himself, wiped the sand from his naked body, and wrapped himself gratefully in it.

"Thanks," he said, dryly.

Suddenly the similarity between the stranger and me struck Marc, too. He pointed at the stranger's face and then at me.

"Is that you?" Then a few seconds later: "Is this some kind of projection?"

"I'm real enough," answered the stranger before I could. "Projections don't freeze and don't wrap themselves in blankets." He checked out Marc, "And who are you? Actually it wasn't such a bad guess."

"Me…?" Marc looked helplessly over to me: "What the…? Shouldn't he be introducing himself to us and explaining this … um … performance?" And while speaking, he returned to my side. He didn't trust anything that was going on here and squinted constantly down at the pistol.

"Who I am," mocked the stranger, "Wouldn't help you much right now. And as for a name… As I said, I don't have one yet." Then he looked directly at me and said: "Erich, give me a name. Please."

He said, "please," and I remembered how I used to always do the same. The situation was grotesque. A human being materializes in the desert sand, growing in slow-motion into a man before our eyes, a man who just happens to be a copy of my own body as a young man. Our entire supply of water had exploded and now the stranger stood there, wrapped in a woolen blanket, and demanded a name. The whole thing was just unreal.

"Can you read my thoughts?" I asked.

"Not here. Not unless I do a takeover."

"Take over what?" I asked.

"A consciousness," smiled the stranger and shrugged his shoulders as if he regretted the statement.

"This is all just crazy," Marc interjected. "Just shoot the damn thing and be done with it!" Marc tried to grab for the pistol. I asked him to stop it, explaining that we were the only witnesses to what was probably a unique experiment. We would find out soon enough what was going on, and until that time he should calm down.

"Good idea!" commented the stranger. "If we continue analytically, you will understand everything: one piece at a time. To start with," now he was leaning on the hood of the car, "I come from out there,"—he pointed towards the sky with his thumb—"from a planet that you cannot imagine."

"I don't believe it," I said, and added, "We know of no planets outside of our own solar system."

"Then it's about time you learnt something new. Time for exo-biology 101!" the stranger laughed as if he didn't have a care in the world. "And I'll show you my home sun when it gets dark again."

It was only then that I realized that a glowing red sun had climbed over the horizon and the car, as well as the dunes all around us, was throwing long shadows across the sand. Unconcerned about my dubious expression the stranger explained.

"I was brought here by the impulse, and that must have come from you," he pointed at me, "otherwise I wouldn't have ended up a younger version of you…"

Marc interrupted excitedly: "This is all bull! He's making up some crap and we're listening like school kids!"

The stranger's face took on a serious expression. I had used to look like that when I was trying to explain something important. He looked Marc and me both in the eyes, one after the other and said:

"I *cannot* lie!"

A moment later, after a pause in which it seemed we could have heard even the lightest breeze if there had been one, he asked again: "Give me a name, please."

Seeing as I didn't answer because I was still busy trying to sort out my crazy thoughts, the stranger continued:

"You have two forenames. You are called Erich Anton von Däniken. You could give me your second forename."

"*What*?" Marc broke in, "You're called Erich Anton? Toni?"

"I never use my second name," I replied. "As far as I'm concerned," I pointed at the stranger, "he can have it. He can be Toni."

"Rubbish!" cried Marc, "Toni sounds like some kind of stolid, upright, Alpine farmer's name. Tomy is much better."

"Whatever. Tomy is fine by me." Then, I meant it mockingly, I shrugged my shoulders and nodded my head towards the stranger in the blanket: "I hereby name you Tomy! Happy?"

"Accepted!" Tomy replied and smiled an expansive smile, displaying 'my' broad incisors, which I no longer had, at least as sweetly as I had done thirty years earlier.

Then there was a moment's silence and we all stared at each other goofily. Until Marc asked:

"So, when are you gonna disappear back into thin air?" Marc was getting more brazen.

"That might take a while," grumbled Tomy coolly. "I am a human being, like you. And this body," he pointed with both his hands at his chest, grimacing as if the body was repugnant to him, "will die some day."

"Can you do magic, or fly, or something like that? Like Superman?" asked Marc, somewhat contemptuously.

"No," answered Tomy with a smile and a hint of superciliousness. "But I can take over being like you. I had to do it to Erich for a short time—or do you think we speak Swiss German on my planet? Everything that Erich knew up until the age of … um … 22 years, four months and 24 days, I know too. The rest is somewhat patchy. And, of course, I know some things from where I come from."

He still stood by the car door, the yellow-brown blanket hanging over his left shoulder like a tunic. The sun was now casting a mixture of crimson light and black shadows over the fantastic scene. Tomy repeatedly looked over to me as if he wanted to say: do you finally understand? Idiot! But he said nothing. Then I had the idea of giving him something to eat. Not out of pity, but simply to check if his body really was human. I was still holding the pistol, a ten-round SIG with the safety off, in my right hand, even if it was only pointed at the ground now. I asked Marc to fetch me a can of tuna from our provisions. I threw it over to Tomy and told him to eat.

"And how am I supposed to open the can?"

Marc dug the can opener out of a backpack and threw it over to land at Tomy's feet.

"He doesn't like me," Tomy said grinning casually in Marc's direction. He opened the can by propping it on the hood and working at it with the opener.

"And what about a knife and fork?" Tomy made the same helpless gesture that I still make in such situations. Fingers spread, palms upwards, shoulders raised. I put the safety back on the pistol and shoved it in the pocket of my grey jeans, which I had been sleeping in on the roof of the car, and fetched him a fork. I hesitated for a second and then overcame my reluctance, walked over to Tomy and handed him the fork, a cheap camping fork. While Tomy reluctantly swallowed the first mouthful, Marc, who was still standing three meters away from us, remarked, "Can we touch him?"

I cautiously touched the left temple of my younger replica; then I grasped his shoulders somewhat more firmly with both hands. Tomy let it happen. He laid the fork and the can of tuna fish on the hood of the car and reached his hands out to me. I took them in mine and turned them over so I could appraise the young skin. I turned his left hand so the palm was facing down. On the back of his hand, in exactly the same place as on mine, was a small, brown birthmark. I looked deep into his eyes and took his right hand. This, too, he simply allowed to happen. This time I took his hand and placed it, palm up, on the hood of the car, which at this time of day had not yet heated up like the hotplate of a cooker. Then I laid my hand next to his and started comparing the lines on our hands. They were completely identical, except that the furrows in my palm had grown a bit deeper over the years.

I was confused and had to really make an effort to concentrate. Everyone in the world is unique—except that I wasn't any more. Here was a copy of me leaning on the door of the Range Rover grinning at me. In the meantime, Marc had crossed over to us with slow, deliberate steps. His cough seemed to have gone and the

29

red blotches on his face had faded. Just stay calm, I told myself, there's a rational explanation for all this.

It had gotten slowly warmer, occasional gusts of wind swirled small spirals of sand around our feet. It occurred to me that in my youth I had had another birthmark that had bothered me so much that I had had it removed when I was 28. I reached for the blanket and pulled it off Tomy's shoulder. He seemed to guess what I wanted, as he let it all happen—albeit with a foolish grin constantly splitting his face.

"Spread your legs—please!" I said, unworried. Tomy placed his hands on the roof of the car and did as he was asked. I squatted down and then I saw it: a small, brown teardrop-shaped mark on the inner side of his right thigh, right in line with his scrotum. I gave up. This second birthmark was the final proof. Here stood my younger double, made of flesh and blood.

Marc asked what on earth I was up to, and so I explained my strange behavior. Tomy interrupted our conversation with the dry observation that the time for gaping at him was over and he would be grateful for some clothes. I had nothing that would have fit him, for at 52 I had developed a bit of a paunch. Cursing, Marc reluctantly dug out some underwear, socks, a pair of black denim pants and a blue-white checkered shirt from the muddle of his suitcase. After he had put everything on, Tomy posed for us.

"How do I look?" After an artificial pause in which he tilted his head and nodded in Marc's direction: "And who's this blond guy?"

I knew that I would have reacted in just the same way. I introduced Marc, but he didn't take Tomy's proffered hand. In a matter-of-fact manner, Tomy pointed out that we had no drinking water and the car's rear window was broken. A quick glance at the map showed us that the nearest settlement was called

Taftan, which was around 90 kilometers away in the direction of the Iranian border. We should be able to manage that distance before dying of thirst. Tomy squeezed himself onto the rear seat in amongst the luggage and I tried the ignition. The engine only managed a stuttering "wow-wow," but wouldn't fire up. The battery must be dead, which I couldn't understand, because yesterday it had been fine. The battery level indicator was registering nothing. I unscrewed the battery contacts and opened it up—there wasn't a trace of water left inside. It was the same with the two reserve batteries, which I had packed for emergencies.

"If we filter some radiator water through some cloth, we should be able to manage a few kilometers," suggested Tomy. However, the radiator was just as dry as the batteries. Not a drop of water left. The sun was rising menacingly and a march of 90 kilometers on foot was unthinkable.

"I'm afraid that this is all down to my appearance," said Tomy quietly. The regret in his voice was plain to hear. "The liquids were all … um … required to construct my body."

I said nothing, and even Marc stayed silent for the moment. He seemed not to like Tomy very much, and the stranger's very presence seemed to confuse him. I noticed that he jerked away whenever Tomy came anywhere near him. After a short while, he sighed:

"Great. You're going to enjoy a really short life on this planet. And dying of thirst is not the best way to go, I've heard."

We opened all the car doors, but remained sitting in the car. It was the only shade. A light breeze kept the temperature within bearable. Tomy touched my shoulder lightly from behind as he unexpectedly held out his right hand as if he wanted to apologize or say farewell. "Look after my body," he said, "even if Marc can't stand the sight of me. Please." Then he suddenly tipped backwards like a sack of flour.

"Is he dead?" asked Marc unemotionally, as if it meant nothing to him.

I felt a weak pulse and suddenly I realized what had happened. Tomy was fetching help. Hadn't he said that he could take over other bodies? A small glimmer of hope lit up in my mind.

"And what happens if he leaves us in the lurch?"

"He won't, Marc. He's like me, and I would never have left my friends in the lurch when I was 22."

"Are we his friends, then?" asked Marc.

"Probably more than that. And if Tomy is what he claims, then you could be too."

"Doubt it," growled Marc in a surly manner. "The way he barged in here wasn't exactly friendly and you can see yourself what kind of mess we're in now."

We leaned our heads back onto the headrests and waited. Thirty-four years ago, I had done military service at the Swiss Army's school for tank recruits. I suddenly remembered one of the daft songs that we had roared out back then after a few beers: "On the tank grave, the roses won't bloom, on the tank grave, the edelweiss won't bloom. The only decorations are shot up old tanks and the hot tears of a girl who cries." Here, 90 kilometers from Taftan in the Baluchistan desert we didn't even have the hot tears. I dug up a few old jokes out of the depths of my grey matter and told them. Marc listened apathetically. After a while, we said nothing more. I thought about my wife and my daughter, Cornelia. I had been married for 27 years and my wife and I had experienced many highs and lows, had some major fights and celebrated sex together. I knew that Ebet—that was my pet name for my wife, Elisabeth—had not only enjoyed the good times with me, we had had some pretty difficult times, too, and financial problems—tax, what else?—which had driven me to the brink of despair. Somehow, we had mastered every challenge, and after my first book, the worst of the unpleasantness was behind us. These days it was less about money, more about malicious critics who slandered me. Of course, there are also those who are correct and helpful, the paternal and the know-it-alls, but they remain in the minority. Really, the best years should have just been starting for Ebet and me...

I thought about Marc's parents and how I had asked Marc to join me on this journey. How would they react to the news of Marc's death? While I was having these thoughts, it became clear to me that I was never going to be in a position to have to explain to Marc's parents that their only son had lost his life. Marc's father, a dynamic sporty type, would have cursed me to all eternity. And his mother, a kind-hearted, industrious woman, would probably have died of a broken heart. My position was pretty hopeless. Marc himself, a loyal, decent lad, was the kind of man who would have fit the leading role in Plato's story about Charmides. Uncomplicated and blessed with a gentleness of heart. Now he sat lethargically next to me.

"Marc," I jabbed him in the ribs, "Are you still there?"

He looked up, changing his position as if he didn't want to be disturbed. "Don't lose heart, kid. We're gonna get out of here," I said to boost his morale a bit, although I was close to losing hope myself.

Our trip had been a journey into the highlands of Kashmir; we had had the Range Rover flown in from Paris to Karachi and had driven from there up the Indus Valley to Srinagar. We had managed to get to all the destinations on our agenda: surveyed the temple ruins of Martand, visited the incredible ruins of

Parashapur, which still today look like a nuclear weapon had exploded there; and even documented the "Jesus tomb" in Srinagar. I had photocopies of 2000-year-old conversations between Jesus and the King of Kashmir with me in the car. One hundred and eighty rolls of exposed film in the cool box...

"Cool box!" I cried and jumped up from my seat. Quickly, I maneuvered Tomy's body to one side and rummaged through the confusion of clothes and destroyed water bottles until I was able to rip open the foam lid of the box. Marc had perked up and looked hopefully over at me with his mouth hanging open. There they were—180 small, black containers floating in a puddle of water. Luckily, they were waterproof. Next to them a two-liter bottle of water—still intact. How could we have forgotten the cool box, especially in our situation? I had bought it especially for this trip and the mechanic in the repair shop had run an extra cable from the main battery to the transformer. The batteries were dead now and the ice had melted and the contents were lukewarm. We took it in turns to take small swigs of water, enjoying it as if were top quality champagne. I sprinkled some of the water on Tomy's face and body to keep him cool.

We laughed. We laughed like happy kids! But happiness is often just a step away from suffering. It was clear to us both that even drinking it sparingly, the water from the bottle and the melted water from the cool box were only going to keep us going for a few hours.

***

I had written fourteen books in the previous twenty years. My specialist subjects, so to speak, were aliens, archeology, myths, and ancient religions. I didn't have the slightest doubt that sometime in the distant past our ancestors had been visited by aliens. They hadn't understood, these ancients of thousands of years ago, and had taken the aliens to be gods. A fatal mistake, which led to the foundation of many religions. Holy, and not-so-holy books, had become the legitimation for countless wars throughout human history, right up until the present day. A sad joke indeed. Of course, I was attacked from all sides, because apart from circumstantial evidence there was little proof, and circumstantial evidence is contestable. Thank God, I had already understood at the time when I wrote my first book, that those who seek the public eye are not only the objects of praise but also the targets for censure and spiteful criticism. I had never expected that the scientific community would heap praise upon me and welcome me into their bosom.

Many years ago, Hermann Oberth, known to many as the father of the German space program, said: "The unjustified criticism must run off you like liquid manure from a marble column!" That made an impression on me! Now, where our will to live was again running riot, I told Marc the story of what had happened to me during the recording of an American TV show. I was sat, back then, on a leather sofa between the professors J. Allan Hynek and Carl Sagan, both of them respected astronomers. The discussion was about aliens and Sagan pooh-poohed the whole subject. He admitted that the possibility of the existence of extraterrestrial life could not be categorically ruled out, but said that such beings would never have any similarity to human beings and the distances involved made the possibility of any contact unimaginable.

Of course, I saw it all somewhat differently—for good reasons—and Professor Hynek took my side, albeit a little hesitantly. He spoke of technologies beyond the realm of Einsteinian physics and refused to deny any possibility, not even the existence of UFOs. Then Sagan patronizingly said to his academic colleague:

"If extraterrestrial intelligence exists anywhere out there, they would have long since opened up diplomatic relations with us!"

Hynek glanced at me and then at Sagan and answered:

"But we haven't opened up diplomatic relations with the chickens!"

My situation was just as absurd. Now I had my alien—and couldn't do anything about it. Who would ever believe that Tomy was an alien?

***

The temperature rose and rose: the content of our water bottle sank. Around 10 o'clock, something occurred to me that I should have thought of much, much earlier. We needed to make a shelter. The sun shouldn't be allowed to shine directly onto the car's roof. Using a tripod from our camera equipment, some rope and adhesive tape we managed to improvise a second roof around ten centimeters above the roof of the car. We did the same thing over the hood. I bent the windscreen wipers up so that they were standing upright in front of the windscreen, jammed the second woolen blanket underneath, opened the hood a fraction, and tied it so that the spring didn't cause it to fly up.

By rummaging around in our stinking clothes, I even found an umbrella on the floor under the rear seat. I jammed that into the window on Marc's side like an awning. Then we took the last few slugs out of the water bottle, as if it were mother's milk. Where the hell was Tomy? And why were there no other cars driving around out here? Admittedly, it was a fairly remote piece of road, but even so, it was marked on the map. Really, we had done everything right. We had started with plenty of water, with three car batteries, with dried fruit and even some raw ham. The Range Rover even had a winch, which was no use at all to us now because it needed electricity to work. And the motor to be running. Marc and I sat around in our underwear. Our improvised roof had an unexpected effect: even though the sun rose inexorably, it remained pleasantly cool in the car.

In my daily decision-making back home, I am a pretty impulsive man. I always know what I want and get worked up about those indecisive people at the deli counter who can't make up their minds. Another bit of that, how about a bit of that one, maybe a slice of liverwurst or headcheese. Heavens above! They make me mad, these complainers, hesitators, these indecisive people who get to the checkout and spend half an hour digging around in their purses, or can't find any change for the parking lot, or go to the shoe store and get the assistant to show them twenty pairs of shoes and in the end don't buy any. I need about twenty minutes to buy a car, and I haven't been to a shoe store for years. And now? It was getting close to midday. All that was left was the melt water from the cooler. Somewhere in the car, I found a roll of aluminum foil. We unwrapped it and laid it on the ground in a big cross as a signal to passing airplanes.

From my time as a boy scout, I could remember most of the letters of the Morse code. Dot-dot-dot, dash-dash-dash, dot-dot-dot was the code for SOS (...– – –...). We laid out clothes in the Morse code signal next to our foil cross. (Later, quite a few people asked me why I didn't just use a cell phone to call for help. Man! In the Baluchistan desert cell phones simply don't work. Anyway, this was back in 1987; in those days, not so many people had cell phones. In the desert, they still don't.)

Where was Tomy? Marc voiced his concern, and it began to gnaw on my nerves, maybe something had happened to Tomy that was beyond his power to influence. Had he landed in God-knows-what dimension? I tried to stave off the claws of doubt and began reciting for Marc a poem about friendship written by Schiller that I had learnt back in my schooldays. Why it occurred to me at precisely that moment, I've never quite understood—even years later:

> The tyrant Dionys to seek, Stern Moerus with his poniard crept; the watchful guard upon him swept; the grim king marked his changeless cheek: "What wouldst thou with thy poniard? Speak!" "The city from the tyrant free!" "The death-cross shall thy guerdon be."

And so on to the end where the tyrant becomes his true friend and says: "Tis mine your suppliant now to be, Ah, let the band of love—be three!"

Tomy was to be our third person, I hammered into Marc. At least our improvised air conditioning was working. I fished a clean handkerchief out of the confusion behind us and dunked it into the tepid water in the cool box. As greedy as young camels, we sucked the disgusting brew down and also moistened Tomy's brows. Wasn't it possible to extract water from the air? I had read somewhere that some Indian prime minister had drank his own urine, but neither Marc nor I needed to go—we were pretty dehydrated as it was. What could we do to get water? Dig? We didn't have the tools for that and we were probably in the wrong place anyway. Should we hang our aluminum foil from the cable of the winch to collect dew from the from the early morning air? We would have had to twist the foil into funnels and put some sort of container underneath every one.

We had four plates and cups in our onboard canteen. Before we could test whether it was possible to extract the steel cable without having any power for the winch, we heard the sound of a distant motor. We held our breath. Was it friend or foe? Quickly we pulled our pants on—I stashed the pistol in my pants pocket after checking that the first bullet was in the chamber. The noise came ever closer, but because of the massive dune in front of us we could see nothing. It was clear that it was some heavy vehicle from the tone of the motor. Thus, it was that each of us stood by our doors, quivering with anticipation. We didn't even notice that Tomy had come back to life.

Behind the dune, the sand swirled up into a large dust cloud. The growling of the engine got ever louder and then suddenly a yellow-brown speckled truck appeared with eight massive wheels and its headlights on. Who would be so crazy as to drive around in the desert with their headlights on? The monstrous military truck drove straight at us and we started worrying that the massive vehicle was about to ram us, but twenty meters before it reached the Range Rover, which now looked like a run-down Bedouin tent with its improvised roof, the driver pulled the leviathan to one side. The truck lurched, covering us with sand and dust, and then came to a standstill.

The motor stalled.

Before the driver climbed down from the cab, I registered Tomy's weak voice behind me.

"Have you got anything to drink?" he asked.

"Only brackish water," I replied automatically and felt so overjoyed that I could have yodeled from happiness. Tomy was back! He squatted upright in the piled up junk on the back seat, looking tired, dried out and asked:

"Has Mahmud arrived yet?"

"*Who?*"

"The driver of the army vehicle!"

"You mean him over there?"

Tomy smiled tiredly. A heavily built man in beige-brown army fatigues and black laced up boots climbed down out of the truck. A wild-looking mustache and 5-millimeter stubble covered half of his face. From underneath his raven-black hair and large, dark eyes with bushy eyebrows poked a beak-like nose from the leathery skin. I then noticed the two pale silver stars on his epaulettes: the man must be some kind of low-ranking officer. Tomy freed himself from the chaos of the car's interior and called to him. It sounded like Arabic. At least, Marc and I understood nothing.

Mahmud, as the bearded man was called, dug three plastic bottles out of his cab and handed them round wordlessly. Before I put my bottle to my lips, I looked over to Tomy, who now stood behind our shattered rear window. He tipped almost the entire contents of his bottle over his head and body before taking a few swigs. Then he spoke Arabic again to Mahmud. He fetched a crate containing 24 liters of mineral water from the back of the truck, 20 cans of cola wrapped in plastic film and a ten-liter container of distilled water. Without saying a word he started untying the cloth roof from over the hood of the car, unscrewed the battery's terminals and began expertly filling up the main battery. Then he emptied several bottles into the radiator, throwing the empties to the floor afterwards and then made his way towards the broken rear window. Tomy said something in Arabic and then asked us to give the stranger a hand. He plucked the remaining bits of glass from out of the frame, took a waxed cloth, and cut it to the right shape using his army knife. Marc and I held the cloth in place while Mahmud took a paintbrush and smeared some stinking black substance that looked like tar around the edges.

After a few minutes, the cloth was firmly stuck in place. Then Mahmud conjured up a battery and jumper cables from somewhere within his vehicle and attached everything to our battery. Tomy, who had been chatting intermittently with Mahmud, asked me to try the starter. The car started first time. I left the motor running to charge up the battery. Mahmud gave us a military salute, called something to Tomy that sounded something like "salaam" and "shukran," climbed back into his monstrous vehicle and roared off, leaving a massive cloud of dust behind.

Tomy's body regenerated very quickly and we silent witnesses, who had stood around like mute boys the whole time, finally managed to get out the questions that we had been burning to ask the whole time.

"Have you got any vitamins and minerals here? We should all take some," began Tomy, before he told us—after taking the tablets—his incredible story.

Around a hundred kilometers from here was the border and just a bit further was an Iranian Army barrack. He had taken over the camp commandant and explained about our predicament...

"Just like that?" snapped Marc disbelievingly. "He just let you come in and take him over and you gave him orders?"

I noticed quickly that Tomy put a lot of effort into explaining things that we found difficult to understand. He was patient: not exactly one of my best qualities. The human consciousness, he explained, understands everything immediately. It is connected with multiple consciousnesses in a kind of network like a holographic image. The problem lay with the ego of the body concerned. This "I" is a world in its own right, created at birth and stretching to the person's present. This "I" is, by its very nature, egocentric, we are all egomaniacs. Somewhere between the consciousness and the ego is a kind of filter. The consciousness doesn't allow information from other consciousnesses—we would say subconsciousnesses—through. This serves as a kind of protective mechanism for the body; otherwise we would quickly go crazy...

"And so you broke through this filter between the subconscious and the conscious and then the ego and—I repeat—started giving the commandant orders?" Marc was determined to get to the bottom of things. He didn't believe a word Tomy said.

"More or less, yes. When someone has a strong will his ego violently resists the takeover because it senses the suppression of his own identity, his "I," and this causes a terrible state of panic. The commander in Taftan is very egocentric and I still have very little experience with people. He is, by the way, from a very good Iranian family and visited Switzerland in his youth."

We said nothing. It was all too much, too quick. We didn't understand and we didn't have the time to sit back and think about it. Therefore, I started picking up the articles of clothing that we had used for our signal and rolled up the aluminum foil. Tomy realized that he was hungry and Marc offered to cut him a few slices of ham. A short while later we were all sitting in the car; we didn't want to take down our Bedouin tent until shortly before we were ready to set off. The battery level indicator was looking a lot healthier, so I turned off the motor. We sat in silence for a while until Marc couldn't hold it in any longer and demanded:

"And when the hell did you learn Arabic?"

"It's just the same as how I learnt Swiss German from Erich," Tomy said. "From the commandant's memory."

It's all too crazy, I thought, that Tomy could take over a hundred people from different countries and he would be able to speak all their languages. Wouldn't that drive him crazy? How could the human brain cope? Tomy's patience with us was exceptional, as I was to learn in the coming days and weeks.

For now, we stuffed ourselves full of ham and crispbread, all washed down with mineral water, but we couldn't help constantly asking Tomy questions. The commander of the barracks, Tomy told us, had only given in after Tomy's consciousness had signalized "no danger" and "good being, friendly being" and the commandant's ego had finally accepted this.

After this had happened, the commandant had listened excitedly like a researcher and started a dialog with Tomy. He had talked aloud, using his voice although this was unnecessary, and Tomy had answered with his consciousness. In Arabic. For anyone standing around it would have seemed as if the commandant was talking to himself, but luckily, they were alone in the room. After the commandant had heard about the situation that we were in, he said that he was powerless to help us—because we were on the other side of the border. He wasn't allowed to send any troops over the border, because it could lead to a political 'situation' and he could be court-martialed and lose his job or even be sent to prison.

It was only after a lot of haggling that he had consented to send a truck and one single officer. If there were any problems, he could always claim that his soldier had simply lost his way. So he had chosen the young officer Mahmud, a mechanic from his division, to take on the mission of helping us. The operation would cost 600 U.S. dollars, not including the water and the Coke.

"Six hundred dollars?" I repeated. "Not bad for an army exercise at the expense of the Iranian Army. And how is he to get his money?"

"We're going to bring it to him," said Tomy. "I promised him. Let's go!"

Resistance was useless. We still had $3,400 in cash and a further $6,000 in traveler's checks hidden in clothes, belts and mats: expeditions can be expensive. So we packed up our Bedouin tent and set off. It was 90 kilometers to Taftan. On the way, I kept thinking about what Tomy had told us. His very presence unsettled me. Many years ago, I had read a novel by my friend Walter Ernsting, who was well known by the pen name Clarc Dalton. In his story, a monk develops the ability to jump from one brain to another. Stories! Made-up fantasies! Now I was sitting in front of a being that really did have this ability. In the flesh and in my own—albeit thirty years younger—body! It was all so crazy! What sort of dream world was I living in? When Tomy spoke I heard my own voice, and that hadn't changed much over the last three decades. Tomy had said he knew everything up to my 22nd birthday and a few months. Could he do everything that I could do? Did he love the way that I loved? Did he comb his hair the same way that I did and would he, over the coming years, develop the same tastes that I had developed? For instance, for Johnny Walker Black Label? For well-cooked chicken? Did he have the same dislikes that I did? Did he hate liver, too? Did he find caviar disgusting? Did beer make him sleepy and champagne make him perky? How would my wife react to him? To an Erich who was thirty years younger? Would she fall in love with the younger me?

How could I explain Tomy to my relatives and

friends? As my father's long-lost illegitimate son? Why would this son suddenly appear now, when he was 22 years old? What sort of stories would I have to make up? My goodness, I had some big problems ahead of me!

"Tomy," I said after an hour on the road, "can you drive?"

"Of course. May I?"

He took the wheel and drove exactly the same way that I did. There was nothing I could have criticized. Normally, I'm like a driving instructor when I'm placed next to young drivers. Now I was in the passenger seat—Marc was behind us, sitting on a box, which we had covered in a woolen blanket. I switched on the radio. Everything was in Arabic. Tomy could understand the voices and translated the Arabic news. I turned it off and looked at him.

"What was all that about this morning with the exploding water bottles and everything?" I asked. "The way you turned up really had us in a panic."

"I'm sorry about that," said Tomy apologetically, "but I really couldn't do anything about it. I can still see you with the pistol in your hand. It wouldn't have taken much and you would have shot me down."

"And then?"

"This body would have been dead; the process would have been interrupted."

I said nothing, because I didn't really understand what he was talking about. Marc picked up the thread and repeated the question about the exploding water bottles and the water. Although Tomy had saved us from dying of thirst, Marc still didn't trust him. Tomy's tone was that of an older man talking to a child. He was trying to clarify certain things and sometimes he just didn't have the words to explain things because—as he said—human tongues had no words for them. After the "original impulse"—whatever that was—had "ignited" his space, the "nucleus had rolled". Energy was the same everywhere. A human body consists of oxygen, carbon, sodium, potassium, zinc, iron, bromine, manganese, copper, chromium, magnesium, molybdenum, titanium, iodine, strontium, rubidium, selenium, boron, nickel, sulfur, arsenic, cobalt, silicon, tin, barium, lithium…

I had interrupted him there. Tomy held the steering wheel in exactly the same way that I did, functioned the same way I did, and could do several different things at the same time while driving; he noticed everything and reacted to everything on the desert track. Marc wanted to know more about this "creation" and Tomy answered as if it was the most banal thing in the universe.

Everything that the nucleus had needed to create the body had been naturally available in the environment, except for the small detail of certain substances in the car, such as the water. To put the body together as quickly as possible, the nucleus had needed more water than the finished body would actually contain, because some of the water would be used up in the chemical processes. He was, Tomy explained, made up of the same 33 chemical elements as we were, his molecules had the same structures, and nothing in his body was extraterrestrial.

"Except for your—what would you call it— spirit?"

"That word doesn't really describe it that well," said Tomy shaking his head while he expertly drove over the extremely rough terrain. "By spirit, you mean the individual, something intangible, immeasurable or, in the case of a haunted house, a ghost. When you say spirit, you're thinking of something like vitality, the soul, because when someone dies you say his spirit has

46

left him. All of that doesn't really define my 'spirit.' The closest I can come to it is 'intelligent energy.'"

Marc shook his head and scratched his blond hair. The more Tomy tried to teach us, the more we realized we didn't understand.

In the distance, we recognized the grey outline of some low buildings, and a couple of kilometers further on we came across Mahmut's military truck blocking the road. Tomy stopped the car and spoke with him. Then he got out and climbed into the truck. We were to cross the Pakistani-Iranian border like any normal person; Mahmud and he would be waiting for us on the Iranian side in front of the barracks. The camp was so large we wouldn't be able to miss it, he said.

I understood immediately what the problem was. Tomy didn't have any papers, so he wouldn't have made it over the border. The commandant had obviously realized it too. So, he was smuggling Tomy, Mahmud, and the truck over the border via an illegal route, while we went through customs in the normal manner. We had what's known as a 'carnet de passage,' a kind of passport for the car, made out by the city where the car is registered. Without a legitimate entry and exit stamp we wouldn't have been able to get out of Pakistan or into Iran.

The Pakistan border crossing consisted of a shed with a straw roof. Four shabby-looking uniformed men with ripped vests and dirty hands wanted to look through our luggage. I offered them a carton of cigarettes, which I had packed especially for such occasions. At last the carnet was stamped, but not before the guard had spat profusely onto the stamp pad to moisten it. The Iranian border crossing, just a few meters further on, was passed without incident, excepting the usual bribes. Baksheesh, it's called in this part of the world. We were probably in the only vehicle that these people had seen the whole week. Taftan turned out to be a settlement consisting of a few dozen houses and huts. At its center was a small mosque, next to it, squatting in front of a corrugated iron shed, were several bearded men wearing turbans. They stared at us in a greedy and unfriendly manner.

I drove aimlessly through the place, hoping that the barracks would soon appear. On the outskirts of the village, we found a run-down gas station with two pumps and lots of trash lying all around. There were old oil cans, crunched up canisters, ripped open barrels, broken axles and everywhere an overpowering stink of gasoline. I needed gas but didn't trust this gas station at all. Who knew what the attendant might be pumping into the Range Rover. Finally, I found a wall, topped with barbed wire with two large concrete buildings behind it. I drove along the wall until I finally saw Mahmut's truck. As I drove by him towards the camp gates, I suddenly asked myself whether we could trust this camp commandant. What would happen if he changed his mind, confiscated our expensive automobile, stole the money, and even had us arrested?

The barrier rose, allowing us access to the site. Left and right of us half-naked soldiers were crouched in the shade of the crippled trees. Directly in front of the main entrance, there was a deck chair where a tanned man in a bathing suit was sitting. In front of him, on the ground, lay an olive green officer's hat and a tin can, which contained the remains of a stinking cigar. His bearded face and black hair reminded me of a young Fidel Castro. The edges of all his fingernails were black. We got out of the car, Mahmud called out something, and "Fidel" stood up. With a look of recognition, he wandered around the Range Rover. All of the doors were open; "Fidel" looked at the aluminum cases containing our metal detectors. I had already told Tomy what was in these cases and he now explained this to "Fidel." He even went into detail, such as how they could detect metal objects at up to three meters deep and in the process distinguish between precious and non-precious metals. "Fidel" nodded appreciatively, his greed seemed to grow.

I recalled the Indian-Pakistani border crossing, which we had crossed three weeks previously. The customs officers on both sides were convinced that every technical appliance was some sort of espionage device. The Indian guard at the Wagah post had pointed with his wooden stick at the aluminum cases and demanded that we open them. It took a lot of talking and gesticulation to persuade him that the metal detector was a broken radio. I turned the volume on the device up to full and—because the car was full to the brim with tools, cans and other metal—the loudspeaker provided a series of squeaking, crackling and whistling sounds which made a pretty convincing old radio. Our "Fidel" here didn't look like the kind who would fall for that kind of trick. He seemed well educated and lot craftier.

We entered a cool room as big as a small gym, which had the Iranian flag hanging from the ceiling, green, white, and red stripes with a red crest in the middle. In one corner of the room stood a large, antique desk; next to it, on a wooden bookshelf, lay yellowing books, which probably hadn't been looked at in years. On a tattered leather chair lay a pile of illustrated magazines with odd corners folded over to mark pages and covered in brown cigarette burns. "Fidel" pulled on a shirt, squeezed into the second leather chair, and indicated a wooden bench on the opposite side of the room where we were to sit.

The cold stone floor made the place seem incredibly clean, for some reason, in contrast to the tired old fans, which whirred and clattered on the ceiling. "Fidel" spoke to someone on the telephone and said, to Tomy of course, that the commandant was currently busy, and then he lit up a stinking cigar and set himself to wait. I did the same with a cigarette.

"I don't like this," said Marc dryly. "This barracks is like a den of thieves." Looking through the windows, we could see the soldiers outside wandering around the Range Rover, peering through the windows to see what was inside. I stood up and went outside: "Fidel" seemed unconcerned. I sat myself down on the steps outside. The soldiers grinned at me but made no move to touch the car. Marc appeared next to me and squatted down beside me and asked what I thought of all this.

"Let's just wait," I said. "The commandant is supposedly an educated man from a good family. And don't forget, we have our own guardian angel: Tomy." Marc looked skeptical. We wandered back into the hall and asked Tomy what he thought of it all. He was convinced of the commandant's honesty. I noticed a rack on the wall with steel helmets and suddenly wondered if these might not have an effect like a Faraday cage and block Tomy's "intelligent energy." He waved our worries aside, saying: "There's nothing that can stop that, not even meshed materials." I tried to explain to him what a Faraday cage was and that a network of metal could cause electrical impulses and radio waves to bounce off itself. But Tomy said I should try to imagine an atomic nucleus the size of a pea. The electrons racing around it would be 100 meters away from the nucleus. I understood what he meant. He was reminding me that all matter consisted of hardly anything more than empty space.

After about an hour, "Fidel" stood up. He had, in the meantime, put on some long pants, done up his shirt buttons and tucked his army beret under his arm. We followed him up some stairs to the second floor. He knocked on a heavy looking door.

The room was artificially cooled, heavy drapes blocking out the bright daylight. To the left of one of windows lay a beautifully colored Persian carpet upon which stood a massive desk. Behind this sat a tall man with perfectly combed, graying hair. He radiated calmness and superiority. On his left arm, he wore a black band of mourning. Somebody he knew must have died recently. When he started to speak, it was in the matter-of-fact style of a newsreader and I could sense his alertness. He was not imperious or domineering and yet the way that he expressed himself left you in no doubt that his orders would be carried out to the letter. At first, he spoke in Arabic to Tomy and then he turned to us and switched to English.

"I have been in contact with Teheran and our embassy in Switzerland to find out a little bit about you. Our religious police are not too pleased to hear you are here, Mr. von Däniken, but you have a valid visa and we will make sure that nothing happens to you."

He waved us over to a group of upholstered armchairs and sent "Fidel" out, calling something to him as he left. Tomy translated that our tank was to be filled up. I pulled out the $600 that I had prepared for the commandant and added $30 more for the cola and the water. The gasoline was on the house, he told us generously, but he would like a favor from us: Tomy's help.

I had known that something was fishy and I asked what form this help was to take. We could discuss it in the morning, he said meaningfully. Now we were to drive to Zahedan, only 80 kilometers from here. It was a good stretch of road and he had reserved rooms for us in the Sahedan Inn Hotel. A jeep would escort us there. The commandant got up, shook our hands, and called for an orderly. Was that it? We had waited around for an hour for this brief audience?

Our Range Rover was back in the courtyard, the windscreen wipers were back in place, and only the canvas rear window remained to show what we had been through. A quick check confirmed that all our baggage was still there and the needle on the gas gauge was pointing to "full."

The first thirty kilometers on the "good" road were not much better than they had been in the desert trip through Baluchistan. We drove past some stony-looking mountains and then, finally, around fifty kilometers before Zahedan the road was suddenly asphalt paving. It had already gotten dark when we finally drove into Zahedan. The place seemed to me like it had been conjured up out of the tales of one thousand and one nights. Clean, paved streets and squares, houses with more than one story, traffic signs, and neon advertising signs. Then a large board: TOURISTS WELCOME AT THE SAHEDAN INN. The empty parking lot in front signaled an empty hotel. As we got inside I caught a glimpse from a mirror next to the reception of an Erich von Däniken that I had never seen before: white hair and eyebrows, beard stubble, dried out skin which looked like red leather, dry and broken lips and a shirt stained by filth and sweat. Marc was dog-tired and went straight to bed. I didn't feel much better, but I wanted to talk to Tomy about the future. He, being thirty years younger than me, had coped with the strain considerably better.

After a luxurious shower, I felt reborn and dressed and went down to wait for Tomy in the foyer. He called down on the telephone to tell me that he had nothing to put on except for Marc's clothes. I told him to come down as he was, as I needed his ability to speak Arabic to go shopping. I changed some money at the hotel reception and asked where we might find shops that were still open. Although it was eight-thirty in the evening, we found quite a few. In no time at all, Tomy was kitted out. He looked good—like the young Erich thirty years ago.

Sitting at a freshly laid table with a bottle of chilled white wine bearing the label Omar Khayyam— after the Persian poet—I told Tomy about my worries. What did these military types want with him? What could he even do? What would happen if we refused? I knew that the Iranian secret service had had a brutal reputation during the Shah's reign and now, under the mullahs, nothing had changed. What would they do if we didn't follow their orders? Or if we tried to flee? Would we be able to keep Marc out of it all? Maybe put him on a plane out of Teheran and fly him home? In my naivety, I thought that the commandant only knew my and Tomy's names, but Tomy reminded me that Marc's passport had probably been registered as we entered the country. So, I suggested that Tomy should take over the commandant again and convince him that it had all been a dream.

However, Tomy insisted that he was incapable of lying. It was enough to make you mad! I suddenly remembered the line from "Hotel California" by the Eagles: "You can check out anytime you like, but you can never leave!"

I can hardly recall the abstruse ideas that I bombarded Tomy with that evening. Couldn't he fetch help from his home planet? Was it possible for him to split himself and take over two people at once? Tomy waved them all aside; which was particularly frustrating for me, because I prided myself on always being able to find a solution for every problem and because Tomy was, so to speak, my younger brother. Only cleverer than me. This thirty-year younger and yet obviously infinitely older young whippersnapper laid his hand—or was it my hand?—comfortingly on mine. Then he suddenly asked what the name of the president and prime minister were; and wanted pictures, too. I went to the reception and feigned admiration of the Iranian system of government—which, in reality, I held in very low regard. The receptionist, who was luckily fairly fluent in English, brought me a brochure with names and pictures. Unfortunately, it was in Arabic, but this turned out to be no problem for Tomy. Then I began to suspect what he was up to.

The next day, I didn't wake up until ten o'clock—I had slept eleven hours solid. Marc was lying next to the swimming pool, and Tomy was sitting at a table studying the Iranian newspapers—after all, he had no problem reading them. I paid the hotel bill and stowed the luggage in the Rover. Two cars were blocking the entrance to the parking lot. They were parked so that nobody could drive past them, however they might try. Two large motorbikes were stationed at the end of the street. I went back inside and the man on the reception told me that a table had been reserved for us for lunch. I had him show it to me: it was set for seven people.

I tried to use the hotel telephone to contact my wife in Switzerland. After countless failed attempts, I finally got through.

Ebet was overjoyed to finally have a sign of life from me, and said she wanted to let Marc's parents know as soon as possible. I noticed a strange echo on the line and realized that the phone was being tapped. So I restricted myself to telling her banalities and made no mention of Tomy. At around one o'clock—I was getting bad-tempered by this point—two official limousines flying Iranian standards on their grills arrived at the hotel. Out of one of them emerged the commandant we had met the previous day, dressed up as if he were at a diplomatic reception, but still with the black armband on his left arm, and then two older, serious-looking gentlemen. They were introduced to me but I didn't catch the Arabic names. One moved smoothly, like a dancer, so I called him Ali. He stank of cheap cologne. The other reminded me of the Egyptian actor Omar Sharif. He smiled constantly in an understanding way with the charming affectedness of a salesman in a bazaar. His charm was captivating; he could probably have even seduced a man into bed.

The commandant, now wearing the khaki uniform of a four-star general, invited us to join him at the table. Us three—the other three—and one place remaining empty. A lady would be joining us, the commandant informed us, but we needn't wait for her before beginning.

We talked in English—Marc had no problems with the language, he grew up in Canada, and Tomy, too, seemed to have no problems keeping up. We started with the seemingly harmless topic of archeology in general and the grand Persian culture in particular. Four waiters and a chef de service flitted constantly around us; it was probably the entire complement of the hotel. They brought a two-pound jar of Iranian caviar, served on a trolley on a bed of crushed ice. It was accompanied by capers, chopped egg, onion rings, lemons, butter, and toast. I can't stand fish eggs, as I've already mentioned, I think they're disgusting. Nevertheless, there's no accounting for taste. For the sake of politeness, I took the smallest possible amount and noticed that Tomy screwed up his face in disgust. For him it was the first taste of Iranian caviar in his life. Marc, the son of a family of restaurateurs, dug in.

The second course was smoked salmon, served with all the usual accouterments. A perfect meal, except that the Coca Cola didn't exactly fit the bill. With every minute that passed I kept asking myself, when these fine Iranian gents were going to let the cat out of the bag. An exquisite, expensive meal just for the sake of small talk? I smelled a rat. Marc and Tomy seemed oblivious. Finally, as our conversation had just steered towards the mysteries of the great pyramids of Egypt, a tall brunette made her entrance, walking a little like a catwalk model. Everyone stood—how well brought up! The woman, who was aged around 28 and had shoulder-length brown hair, kissed the commandant and "Omar Sharif," shook hands with us and stopped in front of Tomy. "It's him," she observed, smiling charmingly at him.

She had a cheerful face, full, sensual lips, and a finely proportioned nose. Something about her bothered me. Was it her self-assured manner? Her lack of concern? The way she treated us like friends? Was it her extremely feminine figure, which was accentuated by her thin, pale-blue blouse? Or was that just because I hadn't seen a beautiful woman in such a long time? Her accent was unmistakably French. Unmistakable for me, because I grew up in the French-speaking part of Switzerland. And, indeed, she introduced herself as Chantal, the commandant nodding and smiling as she did so. She had grown up, she explained, in a small town south of Carcasonne in France and now worked in Iran as a translator for a French oil company.

The third course was served—tender lamb in a white wine sauce with young peas. We talked about hundreds of unimportant and irrelevant things and it didn't escape my attention that sparks were beginning to fly between Tomy and Chantal. Finally, the commandant asked the chef de service to leave us. "Ali" spoke.

"This lad here," he indicated Tomy, "is he your son?"

"No," I answered tensely, "my younger brother."

"Does everyone in your family have this unique ability?" he asked directly.

"No. Tomy really is something special. He always says that he's not of this world." It was a somewhat direct formulation, but the commandant knew anyway.

Silence. Then, without beating around the bush, the commandant said, "These two gentlemen are from the Iranian state security service. I used to work for the department myself. Madame Chantal," he nodded towards the attractive French woman, "is attached to a friendly service. We have been instructed to ask her to assist us."

I was not wholly surprised. Nevertheless, it seemed to me that Chantal seemed so young to be so deeply involved with the spy racket.

"Ali" said that they could provide us with any assistance we might need, but the country was in crisis and they needed our help. There were terrorist groups that were being financed and controlled by persons unknown and they needed to find out as soon as possible who was the brain behind it all.

"It has to be Tomy's decision," I insisted, adding, "of his own free will."

Again, there was silence, until "Omar Sharif" noted, a hypocritical smile dissecting his face, that 'the young man' had no papers and was, therefore, illegally in the country. He said they could help us out with that problem, and as he shrugged his shoulders and splayed his fingers it was clear to everyone what he was getting at. Marc, being a bright young man, realized it, too, and he looked nervously at me. These men could have us arrested at any time—legally. Chantal placed a hand gently on Tomy's arm. It dawned on me that her sights were fixed on him and he had no experience at all with the wiles of earthly women. The situation was tense. I wondered if Marc couldn't jump in and "save" him. Tomy and Marc were about the same age— although in Tomy's case it was hard to tell, really— and they were both good-looking young guys. Being attractive is a privilege of youth. But more to the point, how were we going to get out of this mess?

"My colleague," I said, indicating Marc, "has a valid visa from the Iranian embassy in Bern. I'll have him fly back home from Teheran."

"Omar Sharif" shook his head, displaying one of his disarming smiles. "He is an accessory."

They had us hook, line and sinker. Marc nudged me under the table: I could feel his fist clenched next to my thigh. I could sense that he would just love to tip over this exquisitely laid table in their faces and get the hell out of there. Finally, with feigned diplomacy, I said I could fully understand their dilemma, after all terrorism was not only a problem in Iran. What's more, these Islamic terrorists with their holy warriors were a daily insult to Allah.

"How do you mean?" asked Ali dangerously.

"Just read Sura 2, verse 117 of your holy Qur'an. It says there 'when He wills a thing to be, He but says unto it, "Be"—and it is. He is infinite, omnipresent and almighty.' If he wants something to happen, he just has to will it so, and doesn't need any earthly warriors. To presume that Allah is so small and powerless that he needs the help of fanatics is an insult to Allah!"

"Ali" rubbed his chin thoughtfully; the commandant pressed his lips firmly together; "Omar Sharif's" smile turned a touch more serious.

"An interesting interpretation," he said.

"So it is," I confirmed and then pleaded for more time to consider their offer. I needed to consult with my younger brother. The commandant informed us that the coming evening marked the start of Ramadan, the holy month of fasting. The Moslem faithful were prohibited from drinking or eating, and even smoking, from sunup to sundown. Only after nightfall was the prohibition lifted, so we shouldn't be surprised if it got loud on the streets after eight o'clock. Then he consulted with the two security service men and Chantal. I thought I could tell from their body language that two were in favor and "Ali" was against. Finally, "Ali" gave me his business card. I couldn't read the Arabic writing, but the numbers for his telephone number were legible. With a serious look on his face, he stressed that we couldn't afford to make any mistakes and if we had the slightest problem, we should contact him immediately using the number on the card. There was a 24-hour answering service and they spoke English, he added with a touch of pride. They really need us! I thought.

By now it was around three-thirty in the afternoon and it made no sense to set off now. We said goodbye to the commandant and the two officers from the secret service, promising that we would see them again in Teheran in the Intercontinental Hotel. Although I didn't really have the slightest doubt that some department or other from the secret service would have their eye on us constantly anyway.

We decided a relaxing evening would be the best way to recover from the stresses of the day, but Chantal's continued presence rather spoilt that for me. She had elected to stay with us. Pensively I unpacked the bags from the car and extended our reservation for one more night.

The next day, we met at eight for breakfast. Chantal explained that she would have to leave us as she had to go back to her company in Teheran, but she would meet us there. She gave Tomy a parting kiss, the sort that you only give when something special has happened. Outside a car with a driver and tinted windows was waiting for her. She couldn't—so she told us—come with us, or even go alone. That sort of thing would be impossible for a woman, especially during Ramadan.

Returning to the breakfast table I shuddered.

"Well, little brother how was it?" I asked Tomy.

"The body found it particularly pleasurable," Tomy smiled, "but the experience was enough for me."

"*What?*" exclaimed Marc. "You never want to do it again?"

"Probably not, unless this biological mass," he indicated his body with some disgust, "requires it."

Marc shook his head and laughed. Then he grasped Tomy's hands and I suddenly realized that it was the first time he had touched him since he had come into being. "You can bet your bottom dollar it will," he replied with bright eyes.

We set off a short while later, heading in the direction of the town of Kerman on the edge of the Dasht-e Lut desert. On the way, Tomy explained, as if it was the most natural thing in the world, exactly how Chantal had seduced him. In more detail than we really wanted to hear, to be honest. To start with, she had asked him about his past and he had told what he knew. She had also asked him what his name was, and he had answered that he had none, he was just known as Tomy. She believed this about as much as she bought the story of his creation. The only thing she was willing to accept was that he had a special ability to impose his will on other people, and had gone on at some length about PSI abilities. After 'the deed' he had wanted to tell her about his home planet, but she had just wanted to cuddle and called him "a silly boy with too much imagination." She had advised him to keep both feet on the ground; otherwise, he was likely to have serious problems. "Are all women like that?" he asked. Marc said no—but I was tempted to say yes.

During the long journey, Marc had also wanted to know whether Tomy was something special on his home planet: maybe rich or highly respected. What did it look like there and did they have traffic problems or environmental issues? Which political system did they prefer and how did love work? Was there war or injustices of distribution; what sort of clothes did they wear and which weapon systems had they developed?

The disillusionment was major. There was none of any of that on Tomy's home world. Neither love nor sex; neither weapons nor traffic systems; neither politics nor clothing. Tomy's planet was a place populated by bodiless entities. The only forms of life were the "intelligent energies."

"So you don't really exist?" asked Marc incredulously.

"Of course we exist. As individuals, too. We all have personalities—but no bodies."

"I can't really imagine it," mused Marc aloud. "You have to be born and die sometime, and in between is a life full of excitement. Where does your 'intelligent energy' come from?"

Before Tomy—who was again behind the wheel—could answer Marc's question, he had to brake sharply. Oil barrels had been laid across the road in a kind of makeshift roadblock. Vehicles of all kinds, from semi-trailer trucks to jeeps, stood with open doors, trunks, or trailer doors in two queues. Everywhere, drivers were gesticulating, and in cars women sat silently, wrapped from head to toe in dark material. It seemed to be a particularly thorough check, for the men were completely unpacking their cars and opening up every case, bag or tied up package. Worried, I looked for our passports and for anything that looked like a document that we could use for Tomy. In the end, we chose Marc's driving license.

Two men in black uniforms carrying machine pistols sat in a small truck, which was parked to one side. Behind them, on the opposite side of the road were another two. It took ten minutes until we reached the front of the queue. A young officer, speaking in halting English, demanded to see our travel documents. I showed him only my passport to start with, repeating over and over again that we were tourists. In those days, Swiss passports were issued in all four of the country's official languages: German, French, Italian, and Romansh. The officer seemed not to be able to understand any one of them. He leafed through the passport until he reached the visa, which was in writing that he could understand. Without returning it, he indicated Marc, who was sat in back on a case. Marc pretended to be searching for something and then reached out his driving license. The officer frowned, shook his head, and asked: "Your visa?" I had a sense of foreboding. Marc gave him his passport—Tomy was next. Suddenly we heard a loud whistle being blown. Somebody somewhere called out something.

Our officer strode off towards a dark Mercedes, our passports and Marc's driving license still in his hand. He was clutching them firmly in his fingers, almost as if they were trophies. We weren't in a position to drive off anyway, because of the column in front of us and the vehicles now queued up behind us didn't give us any room to maneuver—that was without forgetting the soldiers with the machine pistols. Oh, God! What would happen if they plucked apart the Range Rover and found our pistol? I remembered "Ali's" business card and starting rifling through bags, desperately trying to find it. But to no avail. I broke out in a sweat. Would Tomy be able to help us out of this one?

Suddenly the officer strode back towards our vehicle, a very serious expression on his face. He pressed our passes and Marc's driving license into my hand, barked out a series of orders, and the small truck in front of us pulled out of the way. Then he began waving his arms around like some kind of traffic cop. Tomy understood what was going on and drove out. I watched as the officer gave us a stiff salute as we drove by him. It seemed clear to what had happened. Somewhere in the column lurked our escort. They must have contacted their command post. Obviously, the Iranian secret service was highly efficient.

Around an hour and a half later, we reached a small town called Na'in, or something like that. It wasn't really necessary to note the name. There was only one hotel in town, the Mahmood. Tomy drove the car into a courtyard that was surrounded by a clay wall. I paid 25 dollars in advance at the reception which left an impression of being a completely pigsty. Untidy, filthy, covered in lumps of God-knows-what and shrouded by some sort of disgusting, sweet smell. A silent, bearded man trudged in front of us up a wooden staircase and ushered us into a room containing around eight foul-smelling figures lying snoring on their wooden-slat beds. The disgusting sight brought me back to life.

Cursing loudly in a mix of Swiss-German and English—it was better that the bearded man didn't understand any of it—I demanded another room and waved another ten dollars under his nose. He said nothing—maybe it was something to do with Ramadan—and led us into another room. This one had four empty wooden-slat beds, and no current occupants. As it smelled of urine and the woolen blankets stank and were probably crawling with lice we decided to return to the car and attempted to sleep for a few hours crammed in our seats between the various items of luggage.

We had hardly dropped off when we were woken by an unbelievable commotion, which seemed to come at us from all sides. The square was lit up brightly with neon light; people all around were talking loudly and laughing; somewhere dreadful music was droning out in awful disharmony. Ramadan. It was unbearable. I persuaded my companions to carry on dozing and drove off into the night, taking the main road in the direction of Teheran. It was a journey of 580 kilometers, but at least the road was good.

At around 4 p.m. the next afternoon we drove into the basement parking lot of the Intercontinental. As I showed my credit card to the receptionist and started digging about to find my passport, he gesticulated towards a corner of the room, from which a deputy manager suddenly appeared, greeting us with exaggerated friendliness. They were very proud to welcome us guests, he assured us. The formalities were unnecessary. He waved over a bellboy, who transported our bags up to Rooms 500 to 504. We couldn't shake off the manager, who insisted on personally escorting us to our rooms.

Room 500 turned out to be the presidential suite and included the bedrooms 501 to 504. All of the rooms were joined by connecting doors. In every room was a bowl of fresh fruit and an ice bucket with a bottle of champagne: the beds were wide enough for an entire girl group. The refrigerators were filled, not just with fruit juices and soft drinks, but also with all the major brand-name spirits. All of that in the land of the Ayatollahs, where alcohol was strictly forbidden, or so I thought. And during Ramadan, too. In the living room was an oval conference table with eight leather armchairs, an upholstered suite and a massive oak desk, solid enough for any state president. Marc whistled loudly and waltzed over to the bed, giggling like a school kid. This luxury must cost a fortune, I thought. But as long as I wasn't paying, I didn't really care too much.

A while ago, I had spoken with Tomy about what we were to do next. I had told him about atrocities carried out by murderous bands of terrorists and he was interested in learning about this side of humanity.

"Aren't you afraid that something will happen to you?" I asked.

"My life-form knows nothing about this state of affairs," he replied casually.

"But what happens if you get killed; if someone shoots you down unexpectedly or poisons you?" I persisted.

"Then I'll just jump into you, Erich, or if needs be into Marc, and if neither of you are available, then into someone else."

Marc took Tomy's face in both his hands and insisted he could come in any time he liked. I recalled the moment after Tomy's creation when Marc had thrown the can opener down at Tomy's feet and Tomy had stated simply: "He doesn't like me." That seemed to have changed, thank God. Understandingly, Tomy said that it would be easier for us and avoid panic and racing hearts if we were to prepare our egos for a friendly takeover.

"How?" asked Marc.

"Lay on the bed," said Tomy and Marc did as instructed. He stretched out, shoes and all, on the heavy bedspread and made himself comfortable. Tomy sat down next to him, asking only that he slide over a bit to make room for him, and if it was OK for him to touch him.

"Dumb question!" said Marc. "Be my guest!"

Almost tenderly, Tomy stroked Marc's temple

with the back of his finger. I was perched on the other edge of the bed and watched as Tomy suddenly went very pale. The blood in his body seemed to stand still. Marc let out a series of short sighs: ah...ehh...ehh... ooh. Then Tomy's body keeled over next to him. Marc grinned and said in a voice filled with wonderment, "It worked! He's in me! Fantastic! Unbelievable!" Marc appeared as if transformed: he was absolutely bursting with enthusiasm.

Although I was aware of how the process worked, I was, nevertheless, astounded and astonished. In front of my very eyes, something supernatural had just occurred. Hypnotism was nothing compared to this. On a whim, I touched both of their cheeks. Tomy's felt slightly cool and damp, but Marc was completely normal.

"Who am I talking to now?" I asked.

"To me," answered Marc's hoarse voice and he laughed mischievously. "With me, too," echoed the same voice right after. Two consciousnesses occupying the same body—without becoming schizophrenic. "Come back," I said to Marc, but meaning Tomy. Marc slid to the head of the bed and lay back. The whole thing seemed to be great fun for him. Slowly Tomy's pasty face began to regain its former color. He puffed a couple of times, moved his arms and legs around a bit, and then sat himself on the edge of the bed. The two looked at each and then began to laugh. They hugged like little children and laughed again, then jumped down from the bed and danced around on the rug. The two had really connected; I was very relieved about that. But now I worried about whatever nastiness the secret service had in mind for us. What we'd experienced up to now could hardly be the end of it.

We decided to take a siesta and slept for about three hours. After waking, we freshened up and went down to the hotel bar where we ordered three glasses of wine.

"No alcohol!" protested the barkeeper, "Ramadan!"

Sometime later, an elegantly dressed man sat down next to me. He wore a dark jacket, white shirt with a yellow-green tie, and grey-blue pants. He was with the 'service,' he informed me, getting straight to the point. We would be collected at ten o'clock the following morning. "All three of us?" I asked.

"Yes, all three," he confirmed.

"Where are we going to?" I wanted to know, but the elegant man simply shrugged his shoulders.

***

They brought us to a large villa in the middle of a park. Probably facilities belonging to the former Shah. We met with "Omar Sharif," "Ali," and three other stiff-looking, unfriendly, and morose men. They were all introduced, but as usual I forgot the names immediately afterwards. One of them was leafing through a stack of black and white photographs of male faces. He asked me how it worked. I replied that Tomy required pictures of the current surroundings of the subject, if possible pictures of the building and the direction of the target from our location. The whole experiment—I used the word intentionally—could only be carried out in our presence. We needed a broad bed, like in our hotel suite, as we required bodily contact. For this white lie, Tomy chastised me with a barely perceptible pitying shake of the head.

As the secret service agents didn't have the required pictures to hand, the group decided to meet again in two days time. I suggested our hotel and the others had no objections. "There's something else," I turned to "Omar Sharif." "We need a passport for Tomy." After a bit of discussion in Arabic, "Omar" asked: "An Iranian passport?" "As a last resort, yes," I answered, "But a Swiss one would be better." More discussion, and then with a grin:

"We have good relations with the Swiss. Your country has represented the U.S.A. since the breaking off of diplomatic relations. We'll see what we can do."

After a guided tour of the city and a visit to the National Museum, we returned to the hotel where we found a Herr Walter Schnebeli from the Swiss embassy waiting for us in the lobby. He was around forty years old, casually dressed and seemed a very accommodating type. He pulled a form out of his black briefcase and passed it to me: "Application for a replacement passport" was written in block letters at the top.

"It's terrible," said Herr Schnebeli, "what happened to the young gentleman. He is your son, is he not?" I corrected that to "youngest brother," which was more or less the truth—Tomy bit his tongue—and started to fill out the form. When I got to the field "Date of birth" I simply added ten days to my own: instead of April 14th, I put April 24th, and I added 22 years to my own birth year of 1935, in other words 1957. In the section "Place of birth" I wrote "Zofingen" and thought, this lie could blow up in my face at any time, because the Swiss authorities at home wouldn't take long to realize that no Anton von Däniken had been born on April 24th, 1957, in Zofingen. The height and weight I simply guessed and the rest I could see with my own two eyes: brown hair, brown eyes and, as a distinguishing feature, a birthmark on the back of the left hand. I gave Herr Schnebeli the form and he remarked what a small world it was, for he himself came from the neighboring town of Oftringen. Heavens help me! I really hoped he wouldn't come with the idea of asking Tomy about his youth.

"And now four photos," said Herr Schnebeli in the friendly tone of a helpful civil servant. "You could be twins," he added, and Tomy smiled. "Only the age difference and the teeth keep you apart." The man was very observant. Tomy showed his front teeth in a big smile. Herr Schnebeli brought us to a photo shop, which was just around the corner from the hotel. After the pictures were ready, he gave us a letter written in Arabic with the Iranian state crest at the top, which had been stamped twice. Two of the photos would be needed for the visa application, he added helpfully, but not until the passport was ready.

After Herr Schnebeli was gone, I asked Tomy what was in the Arabic letter. He said it was an official confirmation that the passport belonging to Anton von Däniken, resident in the Sahedan Inn in Zahedan, had been stolen. They lied in their teeth.

On the next day, the inevitable occurred. Four secret service men and one woman, who we knew only too well, namely Chantal, entered our suite. "Ali" and "Omar" were among them: the other two I had never seen before. One of them was introduced as a doctor. To start with, they laid a picture of a bearded man on the table; then an aerial picture of a city; a close-up picture of a house and a geographical map scaled 1 to 5000 with an arrow over a building. Tomy glanced quickly at the pictures, as if it had nothing at all to do with him. Then he stretched himself out on the bed. Marc lay down next to him. I knelt in front of the bed. We all held hands, a situation that was met with a look from Tomy that said: You're all completely mad. A few seconds later he was gone. The doctor established that his pulse was weak, but stable, and his blood pressure had dropped considerably. He shined a light into Tomy's eyes and observed the reaction of his pupils. Chantal was breathing loudly and deeply: she stared uninterruptedly at Tomy's body. It seemed to me as if her eyes were about to fall out. Sweat was running down her forehead in tiny rivulets. The others, too, were staring at Tomy's pale body as if mesmerized.

Three minutes later, he was back. Marc and I already knew how this worked: the others held their breath in mute fascination. But what was up with Chantal? Hurriedly, she turned away, went off, and shut herself in the bathroom. Tomy stretched and then sat up and said something in Arabic. Now *we* held our breath. The secret service men all began talking at the same time, and I wanted to know from Tomy what he had told them.

"Ach, nothing much. The name of the man that I just visited," he answered, as if it were the most banal thing in the world, "what he does for a living and that he has nothing whatsoever to do with terrorism."

"Incredible!" Chantal exclaimed—she had reappeared from the bathroom and had clearly managed to regain her composure. She bent over Tomy and wanted to kiss him. He escaped her attentions by quickly turning his head away.

"He's exhausted," I said to her, and Tomy looked up at me with dark eyes. Liar! he seemed to be saying to me. Later I found out that the procedure was not in the slightest bit tiring for him. He found it interesting to meet new and interesting people, but that was about to change.

After the sixth attempt, after Tomy had babbled out his report in Arabic, "Ali" ran to the nearest telephone. The whole cabal of secret service operatives, including Chantal, was shouting at the same time. She gathered up her papers and left the suite in a seeming panic.

"What the hell happened?" asked Marc, concerned.

"A well-known, high-ranking religious leader," answered Tomy, and now I really felt that he looked exhausted. "A man so loaded with falsehood and lies that it makes this body, and me in it, want to be sick!" He looked up at us, helplessly. "What kind of awful beings are you? Erich, are there many like that?"

I didn't want to lie to Tomy, and he probably would have seen straight through any falsehood anyway and been horribly disappointed. Maybe he would have even left us. So, I explained a little about the lies in politics, religion and even in science. Marc grasped the situation and began to uncork a bottle of champagne.

"This'll do that body some good," he said.

It did us all good. Right up to the third bottle.

While we were appreciatively serving ourselves champagne, I tried to explain some more to Tomy about our lying society. I mentioned how sometimes small lies were a lot less harmful than the truth. How the truth could sometimes injure people and cause them pain. I tried hard to explain the difference between the brutal truth, the injurious truth, and a white lie. I wanted him to understand why a white lie could be more merciful than the cold, hard facts, and how people could lie with gestures and facial expressions without even saying a word. I wanted to tell him the grown-up lies about Santa Claus and the Easter Bunny, but he knew about those already from my memory. Tomy seemed resigned and disappointed.

At some stage, Chantal called. She wanted to come to see Tomy, but he had no desire to see her and asked her to leave him alone. I was worried about him, but the next day the crisis seemed to be over.

Since the secret service agents left us in peace, we

decided to look around Teheran on our own. We hailed a cab and set off. Every hundred meters or so groups of people on the sidewalk called out something to the taxi driver. A broad-shouldered man accompanied by a woman wrapped from head to toe in a long black burqa squeezed in next to us on the back seat. Two hundred meters further along the road: a student hopped in and took the tiny seat between the driver and me. My protests that I had booked the taxi for us alone fell on deaf ears. He didn't understand a word. The student explained: the people were shouting where they wanted to go to the taxi driver. Whenever there was room in a taxi that was going in the right direction, the driver had to take the people with him. Taxi rides with only one or two people were not permitted, even in a country overflowing with oil!

I wasn't overly impressed with the city. It was too loud, too dirty, and too hot. On top of that, were the half-mummified women—dreadful! So, we returned to the hotel. I remembered that we had a broken rear window in the car so I went to the concierge and asked him to look up the address of the nearest *British Leyland* representative. A short while later, as I drove out of the hotel garage, I noticed that another car was following us. How could I have been so naïve as to think that the secret service was finished with us?

***

On the following morning, we had another "session" in our suite. This time there were two more people from the "service" present. This time, in front of six witnesses, Tomy again scored a direct hit. The excitement among the gentlemen of the secret service was unbelievable. I took "Omar" to one side and made it clear to him that Tomy was close to exhaustion and that we wanted to continue with our journey. What was more, I added, the whole thing was dangerous for us. He, "Omar," kept bringing ever more new faces and the circle of witnesses to Tomy's ability was getting ever bigger.

"What happens when one of these people turns out to be a bad egg?" I asked.

"Omar's" perpetual smile never wavered: that was impossible, he assured me, because only the best of the best had been informed.

"And what about that Ayatollah?" I insisted. "And the Saudi Arabian oil baron that we just met?"

"Omar" shook his head and promised that the service would look into my request.

"But for all our sakes," I urged. "A dead Tomy is no good for you, and we shouldn't do anything to ruin the excellent relations between Switzerland and Iran. And," this was the icing on the cake, "we would help you more, if it was against bands of murderers. What we've given you so far has busted the ring you were after, hasn't it?"

"Omar" shook his head, grinning as ever. This was presumably supposed to display his "appreciation" of our plight. And, while I thought I had bargained pretty well with him, in the eyes of the secret service people I had behaved like an inexperienced fool. But I didn't find that out until later—much, much later.

That evening, Herr Schnebeli brought Tomy's passport. If he had known that his embassy had just made out the first ever passport for an extra-terrestrial he would have flipped.

***

The next day Chantal turned up and asked Tomy to check out just three more people, and then we could

73

go. I gave her Tomy's passport and told her, we would only play along if "the service" could provide us with a clean exit visa. "No tricks, please. For Tomy's sake."

Everything worked out surprisingly well. A little less than three hours later Tomy was again clutching his passport, this time complete with exit visa. Four secret service men were again stood around Tomy's bed: Marc, Tomy and I were holding hands and I fervently hoped that the others would believe that Tomy's ability wouldn't work otherwise. We didn't score any direct hits this time. At the end of the session, one of the men introduced himself as a physicist. He had a request—namely that Tomy should take him over under more strenuous conditions. Tomy shrugged his shoulders and said there were no strenuous conditions for him, but the physicist didn't believe him. He pulled out a fine-mesh steel helmet, bent it into shape, and pulled it over his head, past his ears and nose. I whispered to Tomy that he should punish the physicist a little and make him run around the table a few times. We got back into our positions, Marc and I holding Tomy's hands as he lay back on the bed. As Tomy began to lose color, the physicist began to scream. Then he burst up from his chair and ran around the table five times. His companions fled in shock out of his way. The physicist, holding his mesh helmet like a stretched crown of thorns, staggered back into the bedroom and said, in his own voice: "I am overwhelmed. That's enough."

Tomy returned to his own body and then we all gathered around the conference table. The physicist dabbed sweat from his brow and instructed those around him that Tomy's ability was uncanny and it was vital that it be researched. He made us an offer of one million dollars a year plus the use of a luxury villa, including staff. He was unable, under any circumstances, to offer any more. Such a talent as Tomy, he explained, had a duty to mankind to place himself at the disposal of science. When we didn't go for his offer and, instead, insisted that we wanted to go home, "Ali" began to make blatant threats. Tomy's ability could be a danger to Iran, he claimed, because he could be compromised at any time by enemies of the state.

Tomy got angry, and so did I. Was this the thanks we got for all our help, I asked Chantal, who looked away in shame. Tomy added:

"I will do what I want with my ability; I will do it when I want and for whom I want, and no power on earth can stop me. My abilities will never be used for liars or murderers. Now, let's bring this unpleasant discussion to an end!"

Ali and the physicist tried again to influence Tomy, Chantal taking the role of mediator. But Tomy headed off to the bedroom and closed the door. By promising to keep in touch, I finally persuade the group to leave. I went in and found Tomy lying on his bed staring at the ceiling, his hands clasped behind his head. I sat down on the bed next to him.

"I should go," he said and looked up into my eyes. "But I can't leave you in this awful situation. After all, it's because of me that you're both here."

"Thanks," I retorted, not without irony. "I was the one wishing on a star to meet up with an extraterrestrial, even if I did imagine the experience would be a little different. Now you're here, and before you zip off home, I'd like to learn a lot more about you and your world. I'm an author and I have a lot of curiosity!"

"Me too," admitted Tomy, smiling again, and he took my hand. He suggested that we should all go off to bed and get a good night's sleep so we could make an early start in the morning.

But before we retired to our beds, I wanted to

know if we were in danger from the secret service. Was there anything they could still do to us? "Not a thing," said Tomy wearily, "I would only need to take over their chief…"

***

After breakfast, at around seven, we packed our stuff into our freshly washed and repaired Rover. I handed in our room key and hoped that we wouldn't be presented with the bill.

Leaving Teheran, we drove on perfect roads through Qazvin, Zanjan, and Tabriz towards the Turkish border. We weren't followed. At the Iranian-Turkish border crossing at Barzangan there was a queue of cars and trucks at least a kilometer long. A German truck driver walking around without a shirt on and clutching a can of warm Coke cursed that this border crossing always added fifteen hours to his journey. Not exactly thrilled by this information, I pulled the car around the endless column and drove up the zigzagged road to the customs house. A uniformed man waved us curtly over. Resolutely I waved our red Swiss passports around as if they were diplomatic passports. The uniformed man escorted me to a desk where an older gentleman was sitting, his tanned, wrinkled forehead reminding me of a barbecue. He flicked through our documents until he reached Tomy's exit visa. His expression relaxed and became friendlier, reverent even. He quickly stamped our passports and wished us a good journey. On the Turkish side of the barrier, we finally felt free…

RELIEF

The wastepaper basket in my suite in the Suvretta House in St. Moritz was overflowing with scraps of paper, notes, and computer printouts. I had been writing, scribbling notes, calling people on the phone and typing for four afternoons and three nights solid. I had called Marc and invited him to come here and take a short break in this luxury hotel. Then we wouldn't have to spend so much time on the phone. Marc is one those mountain lads who was put out on the ski slope when he was still in diapers. Now he could ski like a professional—and St. Moritz with its fantastic slopes was a big temptation for him. He accepted my invitation and I was expecting him to arrive that evening.

When I looked out of the window on the left in my room, I could see, behind the snow-laden fir trees, the villa, which once belonged to the Shah of Iran. It was built especially for him and every year he would bring his family to St. Moritz for a holiday. Mario, the barkeeper, told me that the Shah had always come with an enormous entourage of officers, bodyguards, cooks, chambermaids and everything else that you could imagine. The officers had often gotten drunk in the bar, but the Shah himself had never come. "He was in the hotel—often—but never in my bar!" he protested.

And then the religious fanatics had driven him out of the country, a sad chapter in Iranian history, and the western world had closed its doors on the sick Shah—out of fear of the mullahs. Not even the mighty U.S.A. had taken him in. Cowardly western world, I thought. The politicians constantly rattle on about "humanitarian grounds," but when it comes to the Shah of Iran—who, God knows, was far from being a saint but nevertheless did much for his country—they let him die wretchedly in exile in Egypt.

Many months ago, while waiting behind the Turkish border barrier, I had asked myself the same question that I asked myself later many times. Although I knew the answer, it came back to me now as I sat in my pleasant suite in St. Moritz. Why had we worked for the Iranian secret service? And why had they just let us leave, with so little resistance? By the way—and I suppose this partially answers my questions—since our visit to Iran there hasn't been a single terror attack throughout the whole of Iran.

Good work, Tomy!

In reality, the Iranian secret service had never let us out of their sight. But we didn't realize that until it was too late. And despite despising the secret service and their methods, I hated murderers who blew up women and children even more. I hate those liars, who wrap themselves up in the cloak of their religion, who indoctrinate young children that they will be martyrs and will sit at Allah's right hand, that they are holy warriors and their every need will be tended to in paradise—as if Allah needed their help. Finally, and that was another argument in favor of our action, Tomy wanted to get to know this area of humanity. Quite apart from the fix we were in at the time.

Marc arrived punctually in St. Moritz on the Rhaetian Railway. He took a room next to mine and we wasted no time in wandering down to Mario's bar for an aperitif.

"I've already written 150 pages," I proudly announced, and then asked him if he could read through what I had written and let me know if I left out or forgotten anything. His first priority, however, was to get out on the ski slopes, which I could well understand: the sky over St. Moritz was a wonderful deep blue and the powdery snow on the piste was perfect. He would proofread my material afterwards, he promised.

"And do you remember how they wanted to kill us?" Marc blurted out after his third glass of white wine. Although he was now more than 22 years old, he was still the same spontaneous young man. His constantly hoarse voice and his cheerful expression remained unmistakable.

"As if I could forget!" I replied, "If it hadn't for Tomy, we wouldn't be sitting here now."

"And, God, that bitch Chantal!" Marc continued, "The most calculating, cold-blooded, lying she-devil that I have ever met…"

"You're still young," I said, with more than a touch of irony. He clenched his fists: "She misused me, made a fool of me…"

"You shouldn't speak ill of the dead—if you can't say something good, then it's best not to say anything at all," I said soothingly, although I, too, had often wished that I could have strangled her.

"I can't think of a single good thing to say about the woman," Marc insisted.

"Apart from the sex…"

"It was only twice, Erich. Honestly! Back in the Sheraton in Ankara. God! I could really kick myself for that!"

I had known the whole time. Chantal had tried to get Marc to come over to her side, the side of the service. And to throw Tomy to the lions. Marc may not have been able to resist his hormones, but he had remained stubbornly faithful when it came to betraying his new friend Tomy.

Tomy, Tomy! Where was he now? Marc chuckled. For the first twenty-four hours of Tomy's existence he had hated him, had even wanted to kill him. But after the first takeover, he had begun to love him. "Does it make you gay if you adore another man?" he wanted to know.

"Rubbish!" I said dismissively. "And certainly not when it comes to Tomy. He had special qualities. I admire him too."

"And anyway, it wasn't Tomy's body you adored, but the person inside," I continued.

"Do you remember that first takeover in our hotel room? On that big, broad bed in the Intercontinental?" Marc asked. "Remember the way we hugged each other afterwards and danced around the bed?"

As if I could forget. Now Marc explained to me how Tomy had not just taken over his ego, but had also granted him a small insight into his own personal being.

"It was amazing! I could feel a kind of infinite benevolence and an intoxicating feeling of happiness. And on top of that, there was a kind of massive download of knowledge—as if I had understood ten thousand books at once. Erich, it was indescribable. Man, I'd just love to have that experience again!"

Marc asked me if I had called out to Tomy again. Of course I had—many times in fact—but I hadn't had any answer.

The next evening, sitting next to an open fire, Marc read through the first 150 pages of this report.

He had little to add to my recollections, so we talked about our experiences together until the early hours. There was no need to take notes: I left a small tape running the whole time.

THE HUNT BEGINS

We decided to take a midday break in a small town called Doğubeyazıt at the foot of Mount Ararat. Strictly speaking, the mountain is called Agri Daği and its 5165-meter high peak is covered in snow the whole year round. This legendary mountain lies at a politically delicate location, where three countries meet: Turkey, Iran, and what was then the Soviet Union, now Armenia. I asked Tomy if he knew the story of Noah's Ark. Of course, his biblical knowledge encompassed everything I had learned up until the age of twenty-two, he reminded me, so he knew of the supposed relationship between Noah and this mountain. I explained how Noah, in the 601st year and 27th day of his life had stranded his Ark on this very peak.

"And?" Tomy and Marc enquired simultaneously, "Have you found his Ark then?"

"It's not that simple, not least because the political situation," I explained. "Every time a group of researchers has believed it has found traces of the Ark, they disappear back into the ice. The Armenians consider the mountain to be a holy site. They tell how a Kurdish shepherd boy once found the Ark while searching for a lost sheep. After hearing what he thought was the sheep's bell up around the snow line, he had climbed up higher to investigate. Night fell quicker than he was expecting, catching him completely by surprise, so he crawled into a small cave washed round by melted water from the glacier and went to sleep. As day broke, he awoke to find a crack in the glacier a little more than 40 meters from where he had been sleeping. From out of this fissure the frozen faces of many different animals stared out at him, including a camel, two bears, two sheep, two goats, a pair of each one including gazelles and lions. The lad couldn't believe what he was seeing and was sure this must be some kind of waking dream. He rubbed his eyes and clambered a little way higher up the side of the fissure. There he found large, gray-brown stones arranged in strange patterns. As he got closer to them, he realized that these were not stones but old timbers which resembled the bow of a ship."

Marc and Tomy had listened the whole while in rapt silence, but now came the first question: "And why hasn't someone gone up there to check out the story?"

"Many have tried," I answered, "but listen to how the story continues. The shepherd boy knew nothing of the story of Noah's Ark. That evening, as he returned to his village, he excitedly told his story of the ship buried in the ice. The devout Moslems there didn't laugh at his tale and the village holy man praised Allah, who had given this poor boy the honor of discovering Noah's Ark. A few weeks later, when the weather had improved, four men from the village took the shepherd boy back up to the glacier, but the lad couldn't find the spot. The ice had shifted and the position of fissure had changed completely."

"What? That's it?" Tomy asked, as if he thought I was pulling his leg. "Hasn't anyone been able to find this Ark since then? Something that is so important for your culture?"

It was a long story, and I knew it because I had been on the quest myself at one point. And I warned my companions, but they absolutely wanted to know more about Mount Ararat. So be it. We were sitting under the shade of some trees in a Turkish restaurant; the owner and his family turned out to be very willing hosts. Peppers stuffed with rice, raw carrots, and cucumber sticks were all brought to our table. Then came charbroiled lamb, burnt chicken (which I particularly liked), some kind of chopped meat, braised onions, and spicy chilies. From between the trees, we had a wonderful view of Ararat's snow-capped peak. At this altitude, the land was in bloom; children with wide eyes and dirty aprons watched us while we ate, whispered, giggled, and then scattered, screeching with laughter. I knew from personal experience that children—from Egypt to Turkey—always needed ballpoint pens, so we gave them all we could spare; keeping only a couple for ourselves. I asked the restaurant owner if the children could sing for us. Shyly at first, but then louder and louder, the children's voices warbled a song with a chorus that sounded something like "La- di jahara rashiri all wish el maja ..." After the singing was over, I continued my story:

"So, hearken unto me, ye unknowing children, and hear the unbelievable tale of the Mountain of Ararat!" Marc and Tomy laughed at this and toasted me with their glasses of mineral water.

"It was back in the year of 1887, when a group, led by Abbot Nouri, I think his name was, climbed up the mountain. The abbot was the head of a small Christian community around sixty kilometers away from here. A few days later, he reported to journalists that he had walked through the interior of the ship, measured it and the data corresponded exactly to those given in the Bible. Of course, the journalists wanted to

85

know why he had brought no proof with him, but the abbot, a reverent believer of every word in the Bible, defended himself by declaring that the Ark is a holy relic and no one should take anything away from it. He wanted to climb the mountain again, a while later, but died of a heart attack before he could make the attempt.

"Some years later, around 1916—in the middle of the First World War—a Russian pilot, Captain Roskowitzky, claimed that he had seen a great ship embedded in the southern side of the glacier. Czar Nicholas immediately commissioned an expedition of one hundred men to pinpoint the location and collect evidence. The expedition allegedly did indeed find the Ark; they even measured and photographed it. But, returning triumphantly to St. Petersburg with all his evidence in a leather briefcase, the leader of the expedition was captured by enemy forces and never heard from again."

Now we sat eating our lunch in the shadow of that mysterious mountain which so resolutely refuses to reveal its secrets. I could have told many more stories about the mountain, for in the last few decades there had been several more expeditions. Not even one had managed to bring back any convincing evidence. But I didn't get any further: the restaurant where we were sitting was right by the main road and cars flitted by in both directions, including a dark-colored Mercedes that stood out as much for the honking of its horn as for its excessive speed. Two minutes later, the same car drove back on the other side of the road and came to a standstill next to our Range Rover. A slimly built man who we didn't know climbed out of the car, his eyes obscured by dark sunglasses. He was wearing dark pants and a white shirt, wet patches under the arms. Then, from the other side of the car, a face we knew all too well emerged—Chantal.

"What a surprise," she smiled innocently. "I see you got out of Iran in one piece." Completely carefree, as if nothing had happened and we were old friends, she greeted us all effusively and then grabbed a stool and slid it between Marc and Tomy. Her escort, presumably her chauffeur, disappeared into the interior of the building. I wanted to know where she was headed and she told us she was on the way to Ankara. "And how come you're not flying?" I asked. She claimed she had far too many things in her luggage that couldn't be taken by plane, whatever that meant.

Somehow, I didn't trust this woman. She told us she had some time on her hands, grasping Marc's arm affectionately, and seeing as she could speak a little Turkish, she thought she might be able to help us out a little. I found the offer embarrassing. And what's more, we were planning on making side trips to two archeological sites along the way. Just in passing, and more to distract her than anything else, I asked Chantal what she thought of Mount Ararat and the Flood story. "Must have been pretty much as it was described in the Bible," she answered, "or in the Babylonian Gilgamesh Epic. There you find the same story told in the first person by survivors of the flood."

She was well read, I had to give her that much. But that just made me sit up and take notice even more. I asked her straight out what you should never ask a lady, namely how old she was. After the usual coy guessing games, she finally pulled out a French diplomatic passport from her bag: Chantal Babey, I read, née le 28 juin 1957. So, she was thirty years old. I would have guessed that she was a few years younger than that. Why the diplomatic passport? As a connecting element between France and Iran, she required diplomatic protection, she explained pointedly.

She mocked Tomy gently, asking him if he

couldn't simply jump over Ararat and look for the Ark.

"I don't know anyone up there," he answered evasively. She didn't let up, though, wanting to know if he thought the story of the Flood and the Ark were at all plausible. "It's not impossible," he mumbled. "The continental crust is only 35 kilometers thick: there are stresses and fissures in it that make massive floods of that nature almost inevitable."

"And what does that have to do with the Flood?" inquired Marc. I noted that Tomy reacted far more positively to Marc's questioning. When Chantal asked something he was polite, but cool.

"The surface of your planet is 510 million square kilometers, of which around 361 million square kilometers is covered in water. Press a football into that soup and it has to overflow somewhere."

Chantal broke in, shaking her head: "You keep talking about 'your' planet and not 'ours.' Aren't you a human being like us?"

"That's it in a nutshell," Tomy replied subtly. "I tried to explain this to you already, but you thought you knew better."

Chantal looked contemplative, then slid her chair a little way away from Tomy as if he had suddenly transformed into a poisonous jellyfish. Clearly, she had started digesting the incomprehensible truth about him. After a short moment of silence she asked:

"OK. So what's the name of this planet where you come from?"

"You call its sun Vega. It is the fourth planet." He wasn't prepared to say any more.

We decided to set off; Chantal and her chauffeur close behind us. Beforehand I had arranged with her that it wasn't a problem if we lost sight of each other because we could meet up in the Sheraton Hotel when we got to Ankara. But we didn't lose sight of each other: they stuck to our tail like glue.

The newly paved road took us via Agri to Erzurum, where we took rooms in a lousy hotel because there was nothing else available. That evening I managed to contact an old friend of mine, Ercan Güsteri. He was living in Istanbul and gushed about how incredibly delighted he was that we were there, and of course, he would be our guide and interpreter. He would take the early plane to Erzurum and meet us the next day.

I hadn't seen Ercan for nearly two years. He was a typical playboy, the kind you see in glossy magazines: a natty dresser, raven-black hair, a face that was more than a little reminiscent of Roger Moore, always tanned, slim, six feet tall, Porsche sunglasses, and an Omega Speedmaster a permanent fixture on his wrist. I knew him as a travel guide and hobby archeologist and recalled from earlier encounters that he had pretty nationalistic leanings. A Turkish patriot. I couldn't fail to notice his ingratiating smile as he greeted Chantal with a slight bow and an excessively long kiss of the hand. Chantal reacted like a spoilt poodle, wagging its tail enthusiastically around the legs of its master.

Ercan had always been an enthusiastic supporter of my ideas. He had visited me twice in Switzerland and had presented me with large-format pictures of recent excavations in Turkey. Something else: his father had been the representative of some conservative party or other in the

Turkish parliament. Whether he still was or not, I didn't know.

All afternoon we chatted about the archeological highlights of the route we were currently on. Ercan talked incessantly. He wanted us to go to Hattuşa, the ancient capital of the Hittite people. "And then we really *must* go to Mount Nemrut!" he enthused, gesticulating in its general direction. "It is a holy mountain in Southeast Anatolia, Erich!" he insisted. "You can't leave out Nemrut. We have to go up to the peak for daybreak. Then you will see the red dawn from a terrace filled with mighty stone seats and sculpted heads. You've never seen anything like it!"

It was hard to interrupt this cascade of words. Especially seeing as he was enthusiastically backed up by Chantal. I wanted to know if this mountain, too, had its secrets, whether it might have something to do ancient astronomy.

"And how!" answered Ercan and started digging postcards out of his leather briefcase. "There's a pyramid up at the top that no one, to this day, has been able to dig into because the stones just slip back into place. You will be able to take photos of a huge lion head covered in astronomical symbols that no one has been able to decipher. There are engraved images of the moon surrounded by several planets on its breast. But it's the play of colors as the sun comes up which transforms the pyramid and all the seated gods; it's an unforgettable experience. You have to go up there, Erich!"

***

The next morning, after only a few hours of sleep, we set off at six a.m. Ercan had rented a Russian Jeep copy, a Lada, and led the way. We would have all had room enough in my Rover, but Ercan clearly wanted to be alone with Chantal. The route took us past a Qur'an school from the 13th century and the archeological museum being built next to it. Then we were out of the provincial capital, driving through the Anatolian highlands and down into the Amik Plain to Malatya. As the day progressed, more and more trucks were taking to the road, and every overtaking maneuver was like dicing with death. Some waved us by, some blocked both lanes, and the crazy ones swerved out while we were overtaking.

And so it carried on along the E99 until we reached Golbasi. Here, Ercan took a sharp right turn onto a bumpy, unpaved natural road in the direction of Adiyaman. His destination was the village of Eski Kahta, the starting point for the ascent of Mount Nemrut, known as Nemrut Dağ to the locals. The village was right at the foot of the mountain and had nothing to offer apart from a chalet-like hotel, where we immediately booked rooms.

There were no single rooms, only wooden bunks for the military and rucksack tourists. We were grateful to get a room together—Tomy, Marc, and me. Ercan and Chantal managed to get an eight-man room just for themselves. It was obviously off-season and the military seemed to have withdrawn. Later, during a somewhat modest dinner, two mustachioed officers appeared, greeting Ercan like a long-lost brother with kisses and bear hugs. They greet us too in a friendly manner and joined us—at Ercan's insistence—at our table. Their furtive questioning, particularly that of the younger officer, should have made me sit up and take notice, but the heavy, rather sweet red wine had dulled my faculties somewhat. The fact that the officer asked me about my books—which also enjoyed a great deal of success in Turkey—was nothing out of the ordinary. But the probing questions regarding Marc and Tomy; about their relationship to me and what they were doing for me; how long we knew each other; and why they were with me on this trip seemed a little excessive.

Ercan somehow persuaded me that it would be a good idea to take the two with us to the mountaintop.

Because of Kurdish attacks, the region was crawling with military and we would probably have our papers checked repeatedly by patrols or we could even be stopped and not be able to continue at all. It would be cleverer to have the officers on board. His argument seemed plausible.

Back in our room the shower refused to provide our not particularly fresh bodies with anything resembling water and the faucet on the hand basin provided a single water droplet every 15 seconds. We ended up cleaning our teeth using mineral water. By ten o'clock, we were lying on our narrow bunks. A short while later the Ramadan celebrations began. I have never found out why it didn't already start at seven in this community.

As predicted, we were stopped three times the next morning by military patrols, which let us through after exchanging a few words with the officers accompanying us. Ercan, Chantal, and the officers were riding in the Lada; I was clattering along some way behind, drowning in the dust thrown up by their car, which blocked our vision and clogged our lungs. The 'road' got ever steeper and more dangerous. On the right the rocky side of the mountain, on the left breathtakingly deep ravines. There was no room for maneuver. At around 5 a.m. we reached the end of the drivable stretch of the track—it couldn't really be described as a road any more, by any stretch of the imagination. Here, in the cliffs, a small passing point had been blown out of the rock. Ercan turned his Lada so that front was facing outwards, towards the valley, and I did the same with our car. Four hundred meters above was the pyramid-like mountaintop. We were shivering from the cold as we unloaded our camera cases and the metal detector from the car. Then, with our equipment on our backs or hanging round our necks, we set off, still coughing from the dust, in single file on the path up to the summit. The track took us in an ever-climbing spiral. Its slippery gravel, which reminded us of the rusty chunks of rock found between railroad sleepers, made us long for the reassuring solidity of rock under our feet. With plumes of condensation coming out of mouths with every breath, we finally reached a flat stone area that looked as if it had been specially prepared for helicopter landings. We deposited our equipment on the ground. I guessed that this 'helipad' was around 30 x 30 meters. In front of the cone-like pyramid of the summit, we could see the dark figures of five gods sat enthroned on mighty stone seats. They reminded me of the Colossi of Memnon in the Valley of the Kings in Egypt. On the ground in front of them stood two huge eagle heads; a couple of meters to the right were four human heads, all wearing the pointed Hittite helmets of the supposed weather god.

As the first rays of the sun poked their way through the cool morning grayness and began to illuminate this fantastic scenery, we were gripped by an indescribable feeling of reverence. For several minutes, we just stood there marveling at the spectacle, as if it were a kind of natural laser show. At some point, Marc reminded me about the cameras and we quickly began setting up the equipment and shooting as many pictures as we could. The sun poured its ruby light over the terrace and the pyramids in a breathtaking pyrotechnic of color. Two hundred meters higher there was a second terrace with five more deities on ten-meter-high plinths, their gazes directed sternly towards the valley. As the sun illuminated the throned gods on one side of the pyramid with its liquid gold, the other side was thrown into deep shadows. We rushed from one terrace to the next so as not to miss a single moment of this natural wonder. Every few seconds, someone would cry out: "Over here, quickly! Amazing!" Marc, Tomy and I, each one of us armed with a different camera, would run over to whoever had cried out.

Hesitantly, the sun bestowed its warmth on the new day; the dark valleys and peaks around us took on a gently blue hue, occasionally cascading into violet or red. Then the peaks began to shine with white light, which slowly transformed into gold. In the ravines the colors ran into each other and mixed together as if the great master Michelangelo himself were stirring them together for a grandiose composition.

Ercan hadn't been exaggerating. It was a unique experience that everyone should have at least once in their life. In a gallery, arranged from left to right, a stone lion, a monolithic eagle, and then the enthroned figures of Apollo, Fortuna, Zeus, Antiochus and Heracles were lit fantastically. Under our feet, there was a gigantic slab with an engraving of a lion at its center. I could count 19 stars on its breast, along with a rising moon and three planets. Why only three? A short while after the sun had crested the horizon we were finally able to photograph the inscriptions on the rear side of the gods' thrones. The engraving was in pristine Latin letters: Antiochus—who had ruled from 69–36 BC—had had this tomb built for himself and the gods "to leave an unshakeable law of the age by entrusting an immortal message to this untouchable monument." But what was the message he had left on the Nemrut Dağ, 2150 meters above sea level?

After two hours of unceasing photograph taking we had finally ran out of film and were sitting on a mighty stone step catching our breath. Chantal's face looked a little cheesy, as if she were afraid of something. Ercan, on the other hand, appreciatively lit up a small cigarillo and blew out clouds of caustic smoke in the direction of the gods, as if it was some sort of burnt offering. The two officers had wandered off somewhere—at least, I couldn't see them anywhere. The indefatigable Marc was busy unscrewing the lenses from the cameras and carefully packing them away in an orderly fashion in their cases. Tomy was staring dreamily down into the valley, so I went over and sat down next to him.

"What are you thinking about, little brother?"

"Your fantastic planet," he said pensively. "I will have a lot to upload to the community when I return home. They will all be delighted."

"How do you mean?"

He turned to face me, like a mirror image, only thirty years younger. "We have no language," he stressed quietly and emotionally, "My experiences here will become part of the group consciousness. We are all part of it. The Earth is really a marvel of beauty—but you humans, sadly, are not."

My gaze fell to the floor in shame. I took his hand and pressed it gently.

"There are wonderful people, too. Not everyone lies." It was barely more than a whisper: the others couldn't even hear that we were talking. Marc finished his task and pointed at the gravel pyramid in front of us.

"So, what's inside there?"

Ercan explained that many attempts had been made to venture into the interior of the pyramid, but they had all failed. Every time anyone excavated a hole and tried to prop it up with wooden beams, the small stones just trickled down slowly burying the whole thing again. It would take some kind of heavy machinery to make any kind of serious progress, but the track up here would have to be seriously widened and strengthened to get that kind of equipment up here.

"What about a helicopter?" I enquired.

"There's no money for it. And even if anyone were prepared to pay for it, they wouldn't get a permit to dig."

We still had our metal detectors. I started screwing the various parts together and inserted the batteries. Ercan stood up and said he and Chantal would go and find the officers and then drive back down the valley. The military would all be at the bottom of the mountain at this time of day, eating lunch. We couldn't go wrong: just drive down the mountain to the hotel. He shook our hands—which I found a little unnecessary, as we were only going to be parted for a few hours. Chantal hardly looked at us, turned wordlessly away, and walked a few paces across the terrace. Then she suddenly turned around and strode up to Marc, took his head in her hands and kissed the stunned youngster full on the lips. Tomy watched as first her upper body and then her head disappeared into the depths behind the terrace and then asked thoughtfully:

"What was that?"

"The kiss?" Marc laughed hoarsely, "I think she must like me!"

"That's not it," insisted Tomy, a look of consternation on his face, "Erich, what do you think?"

I said nothing and fished for a cigarette. All kinds of possibilities were going through my head. Had some kind of devilment been planned against us? By whom? After all, we were no longer in Iran. Chantal and Ercan—did they know each other from before? I thought back to the overly long hand kiss he had given her. But what would the Turks have against us? Did Ercan know anything about Tomy? It was possible. They had certainly had enough time during the drive here to talk about all sorts of things. Was it something just to do with Tomy, or did it concern all of us? Was the kiss some kind of final farewell?

96

Marc laughed again, "What rubbish! She might be a spy, but if she had wanted to kill us, she had plenty of opportunity to do it in Iran. Why complicate matters to do it in Turkey? Chantal's just got a bit of a crush on me. It's not a problem—is it?"

Not totally convinced, we began taking measurements. The depth sensor spat out its shrill tones at four locations. There was something metallic buried about three meters into the pyramid. But we didn't have the slightest chance of finding out what.

At around 11 o'clock the glare of the sun was beginning to make life uncomfortable, so we started back to the car. We were completely alone on the mountain; there was not another soul to be seen. After we had stowed the gear we got into the car, a little hesitantly. I pressed the brake pedal three times—everything OK there. I released the parking brake and pulled it back on again several times. Again, everything seemed to be all right. I got out and checked under the car, looking for traces of oil. Nothing. Even the air pressure in the tires was all right. The Rover was perfect. Tomy sat next to me, on the mountainside of the car: behind him sat Marc, humming softly. I started the motor and took the first curve carefully in first gear. I had to brake constantly as even engine braking wasn't enough to keep our speed down—it was like sitting in a mountain cableway going down an extremely steep mountainside.

Then everything happened at once. Suddenly, the brake pedal gave way. Quickly, I pressed it several times, trying to pump more brake fluid into the cylinders. Nothing happened. I yanked on the handle of the parking brake. No effect. Normally, in that kind of situation, my reaction would have been to change down the gears and bring the car safely to a standstill—but we were already in first! The great weight of the car and the steep inclination of the slope were making the engine howl in protest. Thoughts flashed through my head: So they *were* trying to kill us! How the hell were we going to get out of this situation?

I yelled at Tomy and Marc that as soon as there was enough room between the car and mountain they should try and jump out of the car. This time the mountain was on the right-hand side of the car, left the abyss. Like in the desert, I again thought about Marc and his parents. The young son dead, and all of it my fault! Our speed increased to frightening levels, the weight of the car pressing it down the slope like a mighty fist. At irregular intervals we skidded hither and thither on the gravel track. I steered the car into the cliff wall. There was a terrible screech and multi-colored sparks flew from the paintwork. How long would the steering be able to hold out? When would the tires burst? I grasped the steering wheel in a bear-like grip; Marc and Tomy did the same with the door handles and the assist grips. The Rover began jumping around perilously. Just don't jump left, I thought. The wheels weren't slowing us much, but the thought of them hanging over a chasm was just too much. For heaven's sake, there had to be a way out of this! A couple of seconds later we flew around a left-hand bend where the rock wall dropped back a couple of meters. Before my companions could open the doors and jump, I cried: "Not yet, wait!"

Just to my left I had glimpsed a tiny meadow with a stream right behind it. In desperation, I tore the steering wheel left, sending the car and us into the greenery. The car skidded across the small patch of grass into the soft streambed and then out the other side, finally coming to a standstill wedged between two extended tree roots. And didn't even tip over.

At first, we just sat there, breathing heavily. Then we all leaned our heads back and sat in relieved silence. Slowly our hammering pulses returned to near normal and we got our breath back.

Marc was the first to speak: "We're still alive," he said, as if he didn't believe it was possible.

Tomy looked at me with an expression that I will never forget. If Mona Lisa had been a man, hers might have been the expression on Tomy's face. Not bitter, not cheerful, not calm, not furious, not angry; simply indescribable.

"The planet *is* wonderful," he said, echoing his earlier comment, "but you humans are appalling."

What could I say to that? Carefully, I opened my door and got out of the car to check out the damage. It was a wreck. Marc and Tomy couldn't even open their doors; the collisions on the way down must have jammed them shut.

"Is anyone injured?" I asked. The others checked out their limbs. Nothing broken, but scrapes, scratches and bruises aplenty and—as we realized later—strained muscles everywhere where the human body had muscles.

We must have had a guardian angel looking out for us. After this rollercoaster ride of terror the car was still standing on all four wheels. The rear door was also jammed, so Marc and Tomy started to pass out the luggage through my door as there was no way we would be driving any farther. I crawled under the car. From my days in the tank recruit school I could still remember a considerable amount about the way brakes function.

Remnants of brake fluid dropped from all four brake hoses next to the suspension mountings. I knew that the brake pedal pushed a rod into a main brake cylinder, from which four lines ran to the wheels. Resolutely I tore one of the hoses from out of the muck it was embedded in. A quick inspection showed a small incision, probably made with snips. The handbrake worked in a different way, namely without brake fluid. Two steel cables ran to the wheels on the rear axle— these also showed signs of being tampered with.

"Who the hell was it?" Marc asked tonelessly, running greasy fingers over the cut in the brake hose.

"Make sure you wash your hands thoroughly in the stream," was my only answer. "Brake fluid isn't oil. It's a poisonous mix of chemicals that can easily be absorbed through the skin."

"Ouch!" Marc dropped the hose and dunked his hands into the cool waters of the stream. "But who was it? That's what I want to know!"

Tomy sat pensively on a rock: "It could only have been those two officers. The others were with us the whole time, from sunup till the time they set off home."

"Not necessarily," I corrected him. "The others may have had no time to do it on the way down, but someone probably cut these lines last night while we were all at the hotel. They knew that we wouldn't be braking so much on the way up and the strain of the slope and the weight of the car would be the final straw for our brakes…"

"Yes, it can't be ruled out," Tomy growled. "But why here in Turkey and not in Iran?"

"And why all of us and not just Tomy?" Marc wanted to know, the fury in his voice barely concealed.

"They are so damned stupid!" Tomy added, "When this body dies I can just spring into another one and there I am again. They can't kill me!"

"But they can damn well kill us!" said Marc with clenched fists. "Why do they want to kill us?"

"We're accessories," I said with resignation. "Don't forget the episode in the Intercontinental in

Teheran. We know who Tomy took over and he could have shared his knowledge about the terrorists and the Iranian secret police with us at any time!"

"Great. So we have to expect to be blown away at any moment." Marc shouted furiously.

"For now, we don't even know who planned and carried out this attack. Either way, we have to get back to the hotel. There's our luggage, our documents and we need a new car."

I realized that we would have to come back to the wreck later: there was equipment and other things in it that were far too valuable to be left here to rot. And anyway, I would need pictures for the insurance back home. So we unscrewed the license plate, pulled up the carpet to retrieve the cash, travelers' checks and the pistol from their hiding places underneath. Each of us slung a camera case over his shoulder and we set off down the mountain.

SUVRETTA HOUSE, ST. MORITZ

The pianist was one of the absolute best, as you would expect in a hotel of this class. A quick request and he would start playing whatever you had asked for. Without any sheet music, I had asked for "As Time Goes By," the evergreen from the classic film *Casablanca* with Humphrey Bogart and Ingrid Bergmann that the poor bar pianist is forced to play every night. Marc's generation didn't know the film and I wanted to tell him what it was about, but he waved my explanations away.

"As Time Goes By, it means how time flies, doesn't it?"

He took a nip from his glass: "How the hell did we ever survive that day on Mount Nemrut?"

"The gods must have been smiling down on us," I answered wryly.

"It's unbelievable," he stuck with the subject. "We're sitting here in the bar of a luxury hotel, slurping down rosé champagne and really we should be dead a dozen times over. Here's to a long life, prost!"

Mario opened a new bottle for us and brought us a fresh bowl of nuts, asking if we were hungry. A young

German couple sat down at a nearby table. The woman gushed on about how she had read all my books. It's always the same, and when I ask they can barely name three of them. This was the case with the young woman, too. We laughed and toasted each other and were simply grateful that we had other guests who we could chat with. We could dwell on our memories later.

"How come you never called in the police? It was pretty clear what had happened."

"Police? Marc, what are you thinking? In Eski Kahta, there were no police. The nearest station is in Adiyaman. There was only one telephone in our hotel and it didn't work, although I've often wondered if that wasn't part of the plan, too."

I was getting going now, the cool champagne—which I drank with ice, to the horror of the snobs—didn't slow me down.

"Anyway, Marc, what would the police have done? They would have asked us if we had enemies and who might have been responsible for the sabotage. They would have impounded the Rover and seeing as the author Erich von Däniken is pretty well know in Turkey the whole affair would have ended up in the papers. Just imagine the headlines! The media these days is a worldwide organism: the news about the murder attempt would travel from Turkey to Germany and then on to Switzerland in the blink of an eye. And heaven knows where else. After all, I'm well known in the U.S.A. and several other countries besides…"

"And not uncontroversial!" Marc threw in.

"And it would have led to interviews. Constant interrogation by clever and dogged journalists, international ones at that. And what do you think would have come out? What could I have told them? The story of Tomy? Don't make me laugh!"

"But you're planning on telling it now."

"Yes, but now plenty of water has flowed under the bridge since it all happened, and besides, I don't know if I'll even publish it. I started writing this story for myself; so I could get the facts straight in my own head. And for you, too. I don't know if the manuscript will ever reach the general public. Maybe in twenty years, and then only as a novel. Twenty years later, there is little that can be verified or denied; many of the participants are no longer in the picture. So people can think what they want."

Then I informed Marc that that afternoon, while he had presumably been racing down the ski slopes, the examining magistrate had called and innocently asked how I was. Then he had gone on to tell me that they had found something, which let me off the hook and confirmed our statements.

"Oh, yes? And what was this sensational find?"

"A bottle of Johnnie Walker Black Label whisky."

"Since when can whisky bottles talk?"

I asked Mario to bring us over a bottle. "See the way I hold the bottle?"

"Yes, quite normal."

"Normal means that I grip it with my fingers. The hand is at the end of the arm and points away from the body. Now when I hold the bottle out and you take it..."

He gripped the bottle and I kept hold from my side. "Yeah, and?"

"Your fingerprints are now next to mine. Fingertip to fingertip but a mirror image. That's what the magistrate explained."

"But what does that prove?"

"Listen. The forensic scientists examined a bottle from the bar in my house. They discovered two sets of prints—mirror images. The same prints! Always mine! Sometimes they overlapped, and that at the same time.

The same person— me!—must have held the bottle at the same time from both sides. You see? If I was holding the bottle out from my body, I couldn't also be the person accepting it. It's just not possible."

Marc scratched his chin.

The pianist was now playing Nat King Cole's *Unforgettable*.

"How do they know that both sets of prints were made at the same time?"

"Search me. But apparently they can prove it. So it must have been two different people simultaneously holding the bottle from opposite sides. My own fingerprints—the proof for Tomy's existence! Things are looking up."

"Crazy," muttered Marc and turned round to ask the pianist to play Errol Garner's *Misty* for him. I love piano bars, especially those with talented pianists and had seduced Marc over to my way of thinking—even though the type of music he normally listened to was quite different. The evening atmosphere in the *Suvretta's* bar was dignified. The music brought back memories and was always at a decent level so that guests didn't need to bellow at each other to make themselves heard.

"How would you have told my parents about my death?"

I did a quick double take at this abrupt change of the subject, but didn't hesitate with my answer: "It would never have got to that. I would have been dead too. But my wife would have had a really hard time with the problem. Thank heavens it never came to that!"

"Tomy should have jumped into Ercan and wrung the truth out of him." Marc said sullenly.

"He didn't want to at the time. And later it was too late."

"It's all so crazy," Marc raised his glass again. "If I hadn't been there myself, I wouldn't believe a single word of your mad story!" He grinned, "Do you remember how Elisabeth reacted to meeting Tomy?"

"How could I ever forget?"

THE MURDER

After a one and half hour hard march, we finally got back to our hotel. Dripping with sweat and exhausted. Chantal was dozing on a deckchair on the hotel patio. At the sound of our footsteps, she woke with a start, regarded us for a moment, and covered her face with a trashy magazine that lay on a footstool next to her. Marc furiously tore the magazine from her face:

"Who was it?" he screamed at her. "Eh? What? *What?*"

Of course, she already knew. The first "eh" betrayed her. I wanted to know where Ercan was. She told me that he had already left, but was she was expecting him back soon to pick her up.

"Pick you up?" inquired Tomy dangerously. "Before we got back from the mountain? So he wasn't expecting us to come back, then?"

Chantal stood up. She had already regained her composure. What had happened, she wanted to know, and why had we arrived on foot? Had we had an accident and should she call for help? Her lying insincerity stank to high heaven. But that kind of thinking didn't help us any. My highest priority was to get back to the car, so I asked where we could rent a car. Chantal spoke to the hotel manager, a wiry man with the obligatory Turkish mustache. Yalcin, he was called, or something similar. After ten minutes' discussion, he was still haggling about money. I paid. I also bought two of the rolls of film that he always had in stock for the tourists. I needed them so I could photograph the wrecked Range Rover.

About a half an hour later, we were again standing in front of our wrecked car. It looked even worse than I remembered. Yalcin wandered around the vehicle a few times and pronounced that it wasn't as bad as it looked. The motor was still intact, the tires too, as well as the entire steering mechanism. The rest could be fixed at any decent repair shop.

"And how is this wreck supposed to get to a repair shop?" I inquired.

Yalcin offered to call a friend of his in Adiyaman who ran a repair yard and had a truck that would be able to transport the car. It wouldn't be any problem getting this high up the mountain with a small truck.

"It has to be today!" I insisted. "And I need a rental car. I don't want to sit around here getting old!"

The truck was there within three hours, but not the rental car. Instead, Ercan turned up. He seemed to have everything under control; he had already heard everything about our "accident."

From whom?

It couldn't have been Chantal; she was with us the whole time and had even driven up here with us to act as an interpreter.

"Accident?" Marc roared, disbelieving. He held his fist under Ercan's nose: "Do you call cut brake hoses and severed brake cables an accident?"

Ercan shouted back just as loudly. If he was lying—of which we were all certain—he must have been a damned good actor. He knew nothing about any sabotage, he claimed, and certainly wouldn't have had anything to do with it. He asked me if I thought he had ever lied to me before. I shrugged my shoulders, I couldn't really know if things he had said at earlier meetings were true or not.

"But haven't I always been there to help you out?" he insisted, and this really put the pressure on me. He really had helped me an awful lot during my previous visits to Turkey. After the heated atmosphere had cooled down a little, Ercan offered to drive us in his Lada wherever we wanted to go and—he stressed this firmly and decisively.

"I will protect you. Nothing else will happen to you here in my country!"

Marc didn't believe a word. I didn't believe everything, but what choice did we have? We were stuck in a lousy hotel at the foot of the Nemrut Daği in a backwater town called Eski Kahta and there was no other transport for miles around. We had to travel to the place where our car was getting fixed and where there was decent accommodation—to Adiyaman. I asked Ercan if he knew who Tomy was and he answered that Chantal had told him everything but he didn't believe a word of it. "Extraterrestrial? Pah! I'd love to have your imagination, Erich!"

"Then you wouldn't object to Tomy taking you over for a few minutes?"

"Never!" he cried and held up his hands as if to protect himself from Tomy. "He might have supernatural powers, but he's certainly no alien."

"And what makes you so sure?" asked Tomy calmly. "Because there's no such thing as aliens. Basta! And even if there were such a thing, there's no way that they would be here. I didn't spend all my time in university studying physics to end up believing in that sort of baloney. Have you never heard of light years?"

Tomy said nothing, just stood there, smiling. I was amazed. This was the first time I had heard anything about a physics degree. And what's more, Ercan had always claimed to be sympathetic to my theories and they are almost exclusively to do with aliens. I wondered what kind of devious game he was playing. I took Tomy to one side and quietly asked him if he could forcibly take over Ercan.

"It's not a problem. But not now. I need to wait until he's asleep."

By the time the truck that was carrying our car piggyback drove past the hotel, we had already cleared out our rooms and loaded everything into Ercan's Lada. As long as he stayed close to us, nothing much could happen. He was hardly likely to put himself into danger. We drove down the gravel road and soon caught up with the truck carrying the Rover. We followed it the whole way to a yard somewhere in the chaos of Adiyaman.

"A perfect location to do us in!" observed Marc, who spent his whole time looking pointedly around for potential assassins.

Tomy shook his head. "I hardly think so. They don't need murdered corpses: they want accident victims." The surprisingly spacious repair yard actually consisted of several yards muddled up together and dotted here and there with cannibalized wrecks. As soon as the Rover was set back down on the ground on its own four wheels it was surrounded by a group of about ten mechanics dressed in dirty overalls, who immediately began a long discussion in Turkish. The owner proudly presented me with his business card: Gürüp Bocörü, I read, Central Garage Adiyaman, and on the back, "Repairs of all kinds. We sell all brands."

It would be no problem fixing the Rover, in his expert opinion. But he would have to order replacement parts from Ankara. If I wanted the car to look like new, he would need twenty days.

I didn't have that much time, and to be honest, I wasn't bothered about the dents and scratches. The main thing was that everything worked properly—especially the brakes. The rest could be sprayed over. Mr. Gürüp convinced me that, at the very least, all four wheels needed to be replaced. They had taken too many knocks and were now badly dented and even cracked in a few places. We agreed on a price of 1500 dollars cash up front. Any extra costs—he generously offered—could be paid later by credit card. He got straight on the phone to the British Leyland central office in Ankara, nodding repeatedly during the course of the call and then proudly announced to us that the car would be ready for collection in four days. A driver would be setting off from Ankara the same day with the wheels and other parts.

"What are we going to do for four days," Marc moaned. "Especially with the company we're keeping." He indicated Chantal and Ercan with a contemptuous nod of the head. "Why don't we just tell them all to go to hell and rent a car to go to all the archeological sites that you still want to visit?"

Ercan had heard everything. He dragged us into a coffee shop across the road and insisted again and again that he had known nothing about the sabotage.

"And what happened to the two officers?" probed Tomy. Ercan explained that they had had to return to their unit; that was why he and Chantal had driven back before us.

That all sounded plausible enough, and yet it wasn't enough. "Ercan," I pushed, "since we've known each other, I have always thought of you as my

Turkish friend. And it's true that you have helped me out quite a few times. But it's also true that you have always claimed to be an enthusiastic adherent of my theories. But back at the hotel at the foot of the Nemrut Daği you made it clear that you don't believe in extraterrestrials. Not in the slightest! Have you been lying to me all these years?"

To my amazement, he kept his cool and didn't lose his temper or appear embarrassed. He said that he found my archeological discoveries fantastic. He thought it was phenomenal, the way I reevaluated myths and holy books and questioned yesterday's world. And he loved my lively style of writing, he said flatteringly, the Turks loved my literature. But all of my discoveries could be explained much more sensibly, without any need to resort to extraterrestrials.

I had a hunch what was coming next. The idea of earlier civilizations—Atlantis and the like.

"Exactly!" he agreed, relieved. "Atlantis lay here, right on our front doorstep, in the Mediterranean. And all the inexplicable megalithic constructions, the huge walls, and all the technology that doesn't fit into our image of the Stone Age— none of it has anything to do with aliens, but rather Atlantis. The knowledge of the Atlantians was employed here, on Turkish soil, before Atlantis sank into the sea. Our forefathers inherited the oldest culture in the world: Atlantis."

This was the voice of the nationalist in him speaking. I was aware of these arguments and knew that they weren't enough to explain anything. My thoughts strayed back to the sabotage.

"If this murder attempt had nothing to do with you and you don't know who it was, then who the hell *was* it? And why on earth *us*?" I was speaking calmly, but very deliberately. Marc sat next to me biting his lip. Tomy smiled, as he so often did.

"Just give me one good reason, just one…" demanded Ercan through gritted teeth, "…why I should want to see you dead!"

"Because of Tomy and his abilities. Chantal told you everything—you said it yourself."

"But that all happened in Iran! What has that got to do with us Turks? And the idea that Tomy is an alien is something I find ridiculous, as you must understand by now."

I was not completely convinced, but I held my tongue knowing full well that Tomy would be taking over Ercan that same night. Then the truth would definitely come to light. But what about Chantal? I asked her directly.

"That kiss you gave Marc, on the lips, at Nemrut Daği. Was that a farewell?"

"What? No!" Chantal leapt up and began shouting. "I didn't know anything about the stupid sabotage, otherwise I would have warned you. And Marc—I just like him, he's a good- looking guy."

"So why were so surprised when we turned up at the foot of the mountain? You weren't expecting to ever see us again. Admit it!"

Chantal explained that she had never expected that the Iranians were going to just let us drive off into the sunset, and she had heard several exchanges in Iran that had led her to believe that this was exactly the case. But she had never expected an attack in Turkey.

"Where then, exactly?" Marc wanted to know. "Most probably back home in Switzerland."

"That's unbelievable! And how are we to be ushered into the next life, then?"

Chantal took a deep breath and calmed herself. She told us that she had never had anything to do with that sort of thing. After intensive questioning on the subject, however, she revealed that contact poisons were often used for delicate cases. An object such as a steering wheel, a ballpoint pen, or even something as innocuous as a handshake could be used to transfer the poison and the recipient died of a heart attack, suffocation, or something similarly unpleasant.

Who thought up such devilry? How could we protect ourselves? Ercan advised us to avoid shaking hands with strangers and not to touch any everyday objects unless we were wearing rubber gloves, or they had been checked out by some other animal. If a fly suddenly dropped down dead, that might be an indication of poisoning. We could also disinfect suspect objects using normal household disinfectants.

"Bloody great!" swore Marc. "And I need a taster for every piece of fruit that I eat? What sort of God-awful situation have we gotten into?"

Ercan attempted to reassure him. Poisonings were not that easy to organize. The agents that carried out that sort of thing had to protect themselves, too. And we didn't have to worry about eating anywhere where other people were consuming the food.

I had heard enough. I was already thinking how I was going to get Tomy and Marc back to Switzerland. Each one would have to take a different route, but there was no airport in Adiyaman. The nearest one was in Malatya, but that was only for domestic flights. What's more, it would be easier to track movements from a provincial airport. I needed a large international hub like Istanbul or Ankara. We had little choice other than to wait for the car to be fixed and to use the time somehow productively.

Ercan volunteered to drive us all to Nevşehir where we could visit the underground cities—it was an offer I could hardly refuse, it was a mystery that I had been fascinated in for some time. He had friends here, he stressed, and to guarantee our safety, he would arrange it so that there was always one car behind us and one in front of us. It was a drive of around 300 kilometers. Plus—he knew me too well—the hotels in Nevşehir were excellent.

"How come?" queried Marc. "Is Nevşehir on the beach? I've never heard of it."

Ercan told us that it was right next to the Göreme Valley with its famous "fairy chimneys." It was a very popular destination for tourists.

Left with little other choice, we decided to go shopping and stock up on some necessary supplies. We bought films, rubber gloves, and new clothes for Tomy. Ercan reserved us two rooms at a local hotel that—like the repair yard—also carried the name Central. Tomy, Marc and I wanted to share a room, we were so spooked. Ercan and Chantal took a double room. After an early dinner we took ourselves to our immaculately clean beds. Before I sank into sleep I asked Tomy if he could take Ercan over.

"Not until they are both asleep," he said.

That night not even the nightly Ramadan racket was able to rouse us from our slumbers. The stresses and strains of what we'd been through, the sabotage, the long march, and all the other unpleasant things had really taken their toll.

When I woke, I glanced over to Tomy. He lay curled up on the double bed next to Marc. Both were breathing deeply and regularly. After a refreshing shower—finally one that worked—I woke them up. Tomy was immediately wide awake, sat up in bed, and shook his head and cursed:

"Damn it! I messed up!"

"Eh? What've you messed up?" Marc turned towards Tomy, bleary-eyed.

"I fell asleep! Plain and simple!"

"I don't believe it," I interjected. "I thought you were an energy form; that you don't need to sleep."

"Yes, but this body does! As I sent out my sensors last night Ercan and Chantal were 'busy' with each other. If I had taken Ercan over at that point, Chantal would have noticed and raised the alarm. Goodness knows who. But that's not really the point. I wanted to take Ercan over without her finding out about it. So I waited and this lump of cells..." Tomy pointed at his naked chest, "...deactivated its waking function."

"Does that mean you're vulnerable when your earthly body is asleep?" I asked.

"My energy form isn't, but this body is."

I asked Tomy to explain more. Tomy told us that a human consciousness needed to be taken over softly; like a blossoming love it needed to be handled with velvet gloves. Ercan had already indicated that he would never willingly allow Tomy to take him over. So Tomy had wanted to wait until Ercan fell asleep and then sneak into his consciousness as if in a dream. Of course, he could also take over a consciousness by force, but this could lead to damage to the persons thinking processes. The victim could become schizophrenic or suffer other mental damage. And he wasn't prepared to risk something like that unless there was really no other choice.

What now? Should we deliver ourselves into Ercan's hands? Simply trust him again, although we still didn't know if he was behind yesterday's assassination attempt? In the end, we decided to risk it, because we knew that we could fall victim to an attack anywhere, whether it was here or on the road. We felt unsafe, wherever we were.

Tomy, Marc and I constantly observed the people around us. A state of affairs that did nothing for our nerves. After breakfast, Ercan presented six new men with confusing Turkish names. We hesitated with the handshakes until Chantal had done it first. Finally, we drove out in a three-car convoy, the Lada carrying Ercan, Chantal, and us in the middle.

The drive to Kayseri and from there via Göreme to Nevşehir was without incident. The roads were good and because we only made a single stop on the way, we reached our hotel in Nevşehir by two o'clock that afternoon. The hotel complex consisted of four buildings which were arranged around a swimming pool and several restaurants.

I noticed a small gray truck parked around ten meters away from the front entrance. It was partially covered in a green tarpaulin and looked somewhat out of place parked there in the shade of several large trees. A lanky man in his fifties with a wrinkled face and the obligatory Turkish mustache stood leaning on the hood of the truck. He was wearing a plastic helmet of the kind that construction workers wear and his eyes were hidden behind sunglasses. The helmet and sunglasses were strangely incongruous there in the shade of the tree. Something about the man worried me. He seemed to be checking us out as we drove into to the hotel parking lot.

At the reception we requested a suite with three beds—we wanted to stay together. I had hardly spoken my request when the hotel director, a tanned man in a white shirt and dark jacket rushed out of his office and greeted me effusively. Ercan explained that he had called ahead to announce our arrival and Erich von Däniken was extremely welcome here. They knew my books and hoped that I would write about their subterranean cities in my next work. It would promote tourism, and that was always welcome. Naturally—the hotel director enthused—the best suite in the hotel had been reserved for us. It had three single rooms for us which all opened onto a central living room. Nobody could come into the room if we pressed in the locking knob on the door handle. How had the hotel director known that Tomy, Marc, and I wanted to stay together and wouldn't want to be disturbed?

We had no desire to doze away the rest of the afternoon next to the pool. Ercan suggested that we drive in the Göreme Valley so we could see at least one of the underground cities. So our convoy took to the road again and drove off into a breathtaking landscape, which astonishes every newcomer.

The Göreme Valley was formed by the numerous eruptions of the nearby Erciyes Volcano. Over the millennia, layer upon layer of volcanic debris consisting of fine ash had settled onto the landscape creating tuff. Wind and rain had washed away the softer layers, leaving the harder layers intact. The result was a kind of lunar landscape covered in unearthly rock towers. The early settlers in the valley had scraped out caves in the towers and lived in them. When the Arabs started attacking the still- Christian land in the seventh century the faithful withdrew to the eerie Göreme region. They were followed later by monks who excavated the tuff rock towers to build churches and chapels.

The interiors of these towers were not recognizable from outside. In the Tokali Kilise Church, where we made a quick stop, we found—behind the modest doors—a magnificently colorful chapel filled with Byzantine frescos. Oil lamps flickered in small niches, throwing their inconsistent light onto the wall paintings. Benches carved out of the tuff stone provided an invitation to sit and contemplate and pray. Even more splendid was the Çavuşin Church from the 10th century. Its frescos looked so fresh and bright that you would have thought they had been repainted every week. Ercan didn't waste a single opportunity to praise the achievements of his forefathers.

Our convoy set off again towards Niğde, which was around thirty kilometers from Göreme. Not far away were the villages of Derinkuyu and Kaymakli, and beneath them the subterranean cities that had been carved out of the rock. Every year—so Ercan told us—new sections of the cities were being discovered. Now they had over 120, many of which were connected by underground tunnels. We parked next to the village church, 200 meters away from a wooden barracks. Outside there was a sign with the inscription "Subterranean Cities." Next to it was a garden restaurant and a few souvenir stands.

Ercan explained that the passages through the rock were often so narrow that it was only possible to walk single file along them. Down to the 14th subterranean level there were electric lights installed. We would see arrows on the walls.

"Those directing you downwards are colored red and those directing you upwards are green," he explained. So all we had to do was follow the red arrows to start with and the green ones to get out again. He suggested that it would be more sensible if he took the tail, to make sure we didn't get separated. We shouldered our cameras and tramped off like sheep following the herd leader, one of the men from our escort convoy. Chantal took a position in amongst the Turks. I had an uneasy feeling. Wouldn't this labyrinth be an ideal place to finish us off? After marching a hundred meters into the depths, we entered a small room with three columns and seats, all carved out of the rock. We took our first pictures there. Marc squeezed onto a seat next to me.

"Have you got the gun?" he asked.

Of course, I had. I had taken it from our wrecked

car and hidden it in a camera bag. After all, we couldn't leave it in either the car or our hotel room.

Clearly, our Turkish friends had never been to the underground cities before either, for their curiosity and enthusiasm drove them on at full pace. They didn't hang around while we were taking photos, but stamped off into the depths, with Chantal in tow. Ercan, who was still behind us, caught me pulling the pistol out of a camera bag and slipping it into my jacket.

"What are you afraid of, Erich? Nothing can happen to you down here." His efforts to reassure me weren't entirely successful. So he began telling us about the underground complex here: the Derinkuyu complex was connected to Kaymakli by a seven-kilometer tunnel. Despite the fact that we were 14 levels down, the temperature remained uniform. He said he would show us the water and airshafts. While he was speaking, a group of Japanese tourists puffed past us, each one of them armed with a small flashlight. Ercan pressed us to continue—the complex was due to close at 6 p.m.

Added to that was the fact that we were due to visit further subterranean cities in the area the next day. So we trudged on, sometimes bent over because of the low ceilings, sometimes even on all fours. We passed through excavated halls that Ercan explained were dormitories, and then supposed living rooms, animal pens, wine cellars, and passages that bent steeply off into the depths and ended suddenly at stone doors that were two meters in diameter. There were wells, air shafts and the odd cross passage marked with two colored arrows: the red ones showing a descending route and the green ones indicating the way up.

Surprisingly, none of us worked up a sweat, as has usually been my experience in such underground labyrinths. The temperature remained constant on every floor. Another thing that struck me was that there were no carvings in the walls, no drawings, painting or other illustrations, and no dates or names scratched into the walls. The builders—or rather excavators— of this subterranean city were big on anonymity, it seemed. Ercan told us that there had been up to 30,000 people living down here at any one time. Per city. That meant that, even if the other complexes weren't quite as big as this one, there had been more than a million souls living in these hidey-holes. Afraid of what or whom?

Right in the middle of our discussion on the subject the lights went out. We were standing right at a crossing and I had just been checking out the green and red arrows. Ercan must have been a few meters behind us, as we heard his voice cheerfully echoing down the passage.

"Don't panic! That happens quite a lot down here," he said. "The electrical system is overloaded and the fuses just burn out every now and again. The lights'll be on again in a couple of minutes."

I rooted around in my pocket between my handkerchief, cigarettes, and some batteries until my fingertips could sense the form of my cigarette lighter. I pulled it out and lit it up: its light flashed against the ceiling.

Marc and Tomy pulled in closer to me. I passed the lighter to Marc and dug the pistol out of my jacket. The lighter's feeble flame was barely enough for us to make out each other's pale faces. I could see that Marc felt the same way that I did—we were afraid.

"Let's get out of here!" I said.

From somewhere in the darkness we heard a high-pitched squeal. It sounded as though it must come from the Japanese tourists. Then a sound of laughter echoed down the passage. It was impossible to tell which direction the sounds were coming from. Above us? Below us? Using the cigarette lighter, Marc found a green arrow on the ceiling.

"OK. Let's make our way to the surface. I'll take the rear, seeing as I've got the gun," I commanded.

As long as the passages were narrow and angled upwards, Marc didn't bother using the lighter. The passage walls were so near that they were brushing against our bodies anyway. And besides, the metal of the lighter quickly became so hot, that it was impossible to hold. Using our sense of touch was enough to bring us quickly to the surface. We panted our way through the labyrinth, which now seemed to us like an oversized termite mound through which we were being chased by unseen monsters.

Every time that Marc discovered a crossing or noticed that the tunnel was starting to go back down again, he pulled the lighter out and used it to find the next green arrow. It was probably only a few minutes—although it seemed much longer—before the lights came back on. Now, despite the constant temperature, we were dripping with sweat and our hearts were racing. In front of us was a small cavern. Was it the same room that Ercan had described as a wine cellar?

"He must be behind us somewhere," I said uncertainly. "And Chantal and the six others must be in front of us; or they took a different route."

We deposited the camera bags on the floor and sat down to catch our breath, waiting for Ercan. After a while, we called out his name. Our cries rang out, echoing upwards and downwards. But there was no answer. Tomy suggested that—with all the various corridors and cross passages—it was highly likely that Ercan had somehow got past us and was already sitting on the surface, sipping coffee. So we decided to set off again towards the surface, constantly stopping here and there for a breather. Finally, we saw a green arrow with a small plaque below it: Exit 100 meters. I stowed the pistol back in one of the camera bags and we trudged upwards, every step that took us towards the lighter seeming lighter than its predecessor.

Directly in front of the exit from the underworld, we saw a garden restaurant and several souvenir stands. Chantal was sitting with the six Turks at two tables that they had pulled together.

"Where's Ercan?" she asked, as soon as she saw us.

"He must be somewhere behind us," I said. "As soon as the lights went off, we lost track of him."

"He knows this place pretty well. He'll turn up soon enough," Chantal said.

We ordered tea and cola and sat down to wait. While watching the Japanese tourists excitedly chattering amongst themselves or buying kitschy souvenirs, I caught sight, in the background, of a small gray truck with a green tarp pulling in between the trees and carefully parking at a particular spot. I stood up, so I could see better. In front of where the truck now stood was a small circular wall. On top of it was a wooden construction with a simple pulley. Three men started working on the well-like structure. They pulled a large circular grill off the top—it was obviously one of the ventilation shafts from the underground city. I watched them lower a rope down into the shaft and then, a few minutes later, pull it back out again, this time with a large metal barrel like an oil drum attached to it. Then a man climbed down out of the truck.

Was I imagining it, or was this the same wrinkled man with the plastic helmet and incongruous sunglasses that I had seen back at the hotel? The helmeted man, again with a cigarette hanging from one corner of his mouth, looked around and gave orders to the men to load the oil drum onto the truck. It was fastened in place; the tarpaulin was pulled over it; and the truck clattered off.

125

What could they be pulling out of the depths? Was the barrel full of garbage from tourists?

A quarter of an hour had gone by since we had emerged. Ercan still hadn't turned up. He was a bit of chatterbox, and it wasn't unthinkable that he had stopped somewhere to talk the ears off some tourists, but it also wasn't like him to leave us hanging like this. I said this to Chantal and she turned and spoke to the six Turks at her table.

"We'll go and look for him," she said and the group got up and wandered off, only to return a few minutes later. "The entrance has been locked—they lock it every night at around this time. One of the watchmen has already done his rounds. There's no one else down there."

"So where the hell is Ercan?" I snapped. "He can't have vanished into thin air!"

We looked around helplessly. The minutes ticked by: the Japanese were now getting back on board their tour bus. Next to my chair I noticed a low, straight wall, which served to fence off the restaurant. I looked over to Tomy and asked him to lay himself down on the wall. He understood immediately what I wanted. So he laid himself down along the wall and Marc and I slid our chairs discreetly over to where he was lying. I told Chantal simply that Tomy needed to lie down as he was not feeling well. She, too, caught on straight way and turned back to occupy the Turks.

"I'm not a bloodhound," grinned Tomy, "but this is about helping someone." Then he closed his eyes.

This time he only went pale for a few seconds before returning to us. He sat back up and spoke the six words that I had been dreading. "Ercan Güsteri is no longer alive."

"Are you sure?"

"Absolutely. Ercan is dead."

Marc interjected: "Did you see his body?"

"No. I can only take over living people. Dead men have no consciousness."

The barrel! The man with the helmet and the mustache. A thought flashed through my mind, but then I realized that it would be pointless to try and find the truck. Even if we had found it, what would we have done with a corpse in an oil drum? But there other thoughts, too. Why Ercan and not us? What had he done wrong?

As Chantal silently began to weep, occasionally brushing away the tears that ran down her cheeks, she finally seemed human. The six Turks chatted excitedly amongst themselves without knowing for sure what for us was already a certainty. Then they went off to find one of the watchmen from the underground city and even persuaded him to open one of the gates and put the lights back on. They all disappeared back into the depths to look for Ercan. But I knew that they would be returning without him.

Chantal sat down next to Marc, who seemed to forget his fury and took her in his arms to comfort her.

"We need to get out of this country," she said quietly. "No one is safe, not even me. Whoever killed Ercan can just as easily kill you or me."

The situation was infuriating. Just keep your nerve and your wits about you, Erich! Our Rover was sitting in the Central Garage in Adiyaman, so I, at least, had to go back there to pick it up. All of our luggage was lying in our suite in the hotel in Nevşehir, around 30 kilometers from our current location. Ercan's rented Lada was sitting in the parking lot, and our Turkish escort had to drive their cars back to Adiyaman anyway. But these men knew that Ercan had crawled down into that rat hole with Tomy, Marc, and me. Would they hold us responsible for Ercan's disappearance? How on earth did we know—they would be asking themselves—that Ercan was dead? Especially in the absence of a body. How were we going to get out of this mess? Notwithstanding the fact that there was someone out there trying to bump us off, too! This person or unknown organization must be well organized and have excellent connections: only professionals could carry out an operation like the removal of Ercan's body from the underground complex so smoothly. And clearly—even if the Iranians were behind it—this unknown organization was able to exert its influence here in Turkey. Ercan's father had been an influential Turkish politician—or maybe still was, as I said, I wasn't sure—which meant that Ercan came from a good family. How would they react to the news of his death? Were we going to have to add Ercan's family to our list of newfound enemies?

I asked Chantal what she thought; plus I wanted to know what sort of connections she had and whether they couldn't organize some kind of protection for us.

She said nothing for a while.

"I don't have a clue how I should go about it," she said. "We don't know for sure who organized the sabotage on Nemrut Daği or who is behind Ercan's murder. The Iranians? Could be. I picked up on a few comments in the office in Teheran. They said Tomy was a monster and didn't belong here."

She scratched her chin, deep in thought, and said, "The Turkish secret police? Can't be ruled out, but why should they get involved? That would mean the Turks were operating on behalf of the Iranians, and in the short time that we've been here that seems unlikely. Or had Ercan's murder nothing at all to do with us? Maybe it was some kind of revenge or feud that only involves Ercan and his family."

"Maybe you should start telling us a bit more

about what you're doing here," Marc noted dryly. "Who are you working for? Who are you getting orders from? And what kind of orders?"

Chantal seemed to struggle with her conscience for a while and then explained to us that the secret services of many different countries kept in close contact. The services worked together when a matter arose that could affect several different states, and Tomy was such a case.

"Why?" I wanted to know. "Tomy hasn't hurt anybody. And even if someone has decided that Tomy is a 'monster,' why aren't they concentrating on him instead of all of us, and now Ercan who wasn't even in Teheran? It's all absurd!"

"Erich, you don't understand the context and the implications," Chantal said quietly and looked directly into my eyes. "Up until recently even I didn't believe that Tomy was an alien. I was thinking more along the lines of superhuman abilities, so-called psi powers. But now I'm starting to believe it. And in Teheran there are clearly many people, several scientists even, who do the same. In their eyes, Tomy is an unbelievable danger to human society. Just imagine! Say he took over a world leader or even the Pope, as far as I'm concerned. Just think about it, Erich!"

We said nothing. But what did Ercan have to do with all this? Chantal revealed a capacity for analytical thinking that I had not expected from her.

"Inasmuch as Ercan really did disappear because of Tomy—which we still don't know for sure—then that's my fault. I told Ercan everything about Tomy and the anti-terrorist action in the Intercontinental in Teheran. Admittedly, Ercan didn't swallow the story that Tomy was an extraterrestrial, but he, too, believed in psi abilities. We only talked in the hotel or in his Lada, but obviously we were bugged somehow. In one or the other, or even both locations. I need to get back to the hotel, have a shower, and then check through my underwear and other clothes. Maybe I'm carrying a bug even now!"

"Bloody great," Marc scoffed. "Then everything we've just talked about has been heard and the 'invisible powers' know exactly what we're planning. We should stop talking and all go and shower and check out our luggage together. How do you find a hidden transmitter?"

"Lay your clothes on the floor and just stamp on everything. You'll hear a crunch if there's anything there!"

One after the other our Turkish traveling companions reemerged from the underground labyrinth. Chantal was clever enough not to let them know what we knew. I didn't understand anything of what she talked to them about, but their questioning faces and gestures all said the same thing: Where is Ercan? Chantal translated for us: the Turks wanted us to wait and what's more, none of us had the key to the Lada anyway. While the sun bathed us in its last few rays the waiters put small wind lights out on the tables. Ercan still didn't turn up. My companions and I wanted to drive back to Nevşehir, to our hotel. One of the men suggested that maybe Ercan had met someone and was having some kind of amorous adventure, and had even driven back to the hotel in another car. The whole group laughed at that idea. Even if Ercan didn't turn up until much later, it wouldn't be a problem for him to get back to the hotel, 30 kilometers away. He knew his way around here. So we decided to drive back to Nevşehir. The fattest of the Turks in our group proved to have hidden talents—he had the Lada open in a trice and after fiddling around for a little while under the hood, he got the motor running. Chantal, Marc, Tomy, and I got into the car; I took the wheel. Our friends, as before, drove in front and behind.

But what would happen now? I suggested that I should drive back to Adiyaman the next morning alone, wait for the repairs on the Rover to be completed and then drive the car on to Istanbul. Once there, I could seek out a customs agent to help me ship the car back to Venice. My companions were against the idea. None of them wanted to leave me on my own. Then I had the idea of sending Marc and Tomy separately from Ankara or Istanbul to some Western European city by plane. To Vienna, Rome, London or anywhere. This plan, too, was not popular. But there was one thing we all agreed on: we should leave the country as soon as possible.

Back at the hotel, I invited our Turkish friends to join us for an evening meal and, as they had all insisted that they weren't leaving Nevşehir without Ercan, I made inquiries about renting another car. It wasn't a problem at this tourist hotspot. Less than one hour later I had the keys to an almost brand new Volkswagen in my hands. I called Elisabeth back in Switzerland, but again took care not to reveal too many details. I told her that we had been involved in a car crash, but neither Marc nor I had been injured—Tomy wasn't mentioned at all. I asked her if she'd paid all my credit card bills, because I would probably need more money. I could get this from the American Express office in Ankara as long as there was no outstanding balance on my account. Back in our hotel room we checked ourselves out for hidden micro transmitters and then laid all our clothes on the floor and trampled over everything. There were no crunching noises. Chantal had asked Marc to help her undress and search for bugs, but he wasn't ready for that just yet.

The next day, the hotel manager informed me that

my Turkish friends had driven back to Derinkuyu to look for Ercan. They had come up with the idea that when the lights had gone out he had maybe taken one of the tunnels that led to the neighboring labyrinth at Kaymakli. Maybe he had fallen, broken his leg and was waiting for help. I knew better, but I said nothing.

My group, including Chantal, decided to take a short detour to visit another archeological site on the way to Adiyaman. It was no good arriving early in Adiyaman if we were just going to have to sit there twiddling our thumbs until the car was repaired. Of course, I had called Mr. Gürüp from the Central Garage beforehand to see how it was going, but he had insisted that they still needed a couple of days. So we left Nevşehir and drove off in the direction of Kayseri where we turned north towards the small town of Boğazkale. The VW proved to have been a good choice, even on the awful roads we now traveled.

We found ourselves looking constantly back over our shoulders, but no one was following us. Just before we arrived at our destination, the road took a steep upwards bend around the mountainside. At the top—our destination—the millennia-old remains of Hattuşa, the former capital of the Hittite Empire. Seen from a distance, the ruins seem to cling to the mountainside, as if they were natural components of the gray cliffs. Then you see a massive dry-stone wall and, emerging from the curved monoliths, two lions with open mouths. At the highest point within the walls was the so-called Royal City, as the archeologists of our time named it. I recalled that in around 1300 BC the Hittites reigned supreme in the region. Their territory stretched into North Syria and they had brought down the Babylonian Hammurabi Dynasty. They had even defeated the Egyptian army at the Battle of Kadesh around 1285 BC. And—just like the Egyptians—they claimed that their kings were gods who had descended direct from the heavens.

There was little left of the former glory. The dry-stone walls, a tunnel through a wall that was around thirty meters thick and below, at the entrance to Hattuşa, enormous monolithic slabs cut into shape and polished to a sheen using tools that we could only imagine these days. I thought back to Ercan's vision of Atlantis. Not far from these floor slabs were megalithic walls, cut from a single piece of stone as though it had been as soft as butter at the time. I knew of similar mighty blocks at other archeological sites, in Abydos in Egypt, in Mycenae in Greece, in Malta in the Mediterranean Sea, but also in Cusco in faraway Peru.

Why, I have always asked myself, did our forefathers put so much effort into creating such monolithic building projects, sometimes dragging the building materials hundreds of miles over mountainous country where they could just have easily have taken smaller stones from the local area and just used them instead? Why is it that the oldest of cultural monuments are also the mightiest? Did the tools or the knowledge come from gods who later disappeared? Did our forefathers master techniques that we today have no knowledge of?

When we returned to the VW, we found an old man sitting at the side of a path just a few meters away from the car in front of a tipped over metal drum. I was so nervous, I almost reflexively went for my pistol. Then a lad appeared, as if from nowhere, carrying souvenirs that he claimed were all genuine artifacts: Hittite knives, figurines, clay fragments, bleached bones with carvings and a cylinder seal. The latter could really have been genuine, but I resisted. Buying anything that was even suspected of being a genuine artifact could land you in serious trouble at customs.

In the meantime, the old man had starting trying to light a fire with split wood, which he had loaded into the drum. He used straw fronds to fan air onto the embers and added ever-thicker pieces as the fire slowly caught. A thin plume of smoke climbed up into the blue sky. Chantal spoke to the old man in an affable tone of voice and he explained to her that he was the guardian of Hattuşa and the rock sanctuary of Yazılıkaya. We had to pay a fee for our sightseeing.

"What sanctuary?" I wanted to know. I had never heard of Yazılıkaya.

The lad led us along the cliff and then through a narrow gap between two large rocks. I asked my companions to keep their eyes peeled, because I was still convinced that something could happen to us at any second, even here. We arrived at a stone room that was open to the sky. There were countless figures carved into the walls: images of gods in flat relief, all with stern expressions and all immaculately carved out of the living rock. The figures carried swords and clubs in their hands, wore pointed hats that reminded me of the ceremonial miters worn by Christian bishops. Then there were complete sequences of images enclosed in a large frame. Above it hovered the divine eagles, at least that what they're called. They reminded me of the falcon-headed Egyptian god Horus, the son of Osiris and Isis. The individual deities in the reliefs clutched objects in their fists that hung down to the floor between their legs. To give you an idea of what they looked like: just imagine workmen operating jackhammers. I knew similar representations from another corner of the world: from Copan in Central America, center of the Mayan culture. So we got out our cameras again and took photographs of everything. Beforehand, I had asked Chantal to stand watch at the narrow entrance and to shout loudly if anyone came.

But we remained undisturbed. Had the "invisible powers" lost track of us? I reminded myself that they wouldn't have any problem picking up our trail again, because we still had to pick up the car from the Central Garage in Adiyaman. And they knew it.

At around 4 p.m. we were back on the road, driving back the same way we had come. We booked into a half decent hotel in Kayseri and apart from Chantal wanting to share a room with Marc, nothing of note happened.

The next day we drove though Malatya back to Adiyaman and straight to the repair yard at the Central Garage. Mr. Gürüp proudly presented the Rover. The repair work had all gone smoothly, the worst of the dents had been hammered out, and the brakes had new cables and hoses. They would spray the car that evening, assured Mr. Gürüp, allowing the paintwork to dry overnight. Then they only had to put the wheels back on and we could be on our way.

During dinner that evening a uniformed policeman asked for me at reception and brought two gentlemen in plain clothes over to our table. They were very polite and presented their identification cards—they meant nothing to us, but Chantal assured us that they were high-ranking officers—and wanted to know everything we could tell them about Ercan Güsteri. How long had we known each other? How often had we met? If he had visited me in Switzerland and—of course—what we could tell them about Ercan's disappearance. We patiently told them everything we knew. Afterwards, the older of the two inquired how long we were planning to stay in Turkey and what would be our next port of call. Finally, laughing sheepishly, he pulled two of my books out of his briefcase and asked if I could autograph them.

"They know that Ercan is gone, but they have no

body," Chantal stated. We speculated as to whether one of Ercan's team of companions had maybe reported him as missing, but these men could hardly have been from the same department that spirited him away in the oil drum.

"I already said," insisted Chantal, "that maybe Ercan's disappearance had nothing to do with us and Tomy. Maybe it was some other kind of debt that was being paid." But I didn't believe that. The expert organization with the truck, the men with the pulley and the oil drum was—for me—just a bit too much effort to go to for a personal grievance.

My plan for the next day was to drive the whole way from Adiyaman to Ankara, around 600 kilometers from east to west. We all wanted to get out of Turkey and to get as near as possible to Switzerland. I called the Sheraton Hotel in Ankara and booked us a couple of rooms. I knew the hotel from earlier visits, and I was also a member of the Sheraton club, which guaranteed me a room, even when the hotel was booked up.

Mr. Gürüp was true to his word, and our car stood sparkling clean and freshly painted on its new wheels as we arrived. Before I got into the car, I asked the garage owner to get in and put his hands on the steering wheel. I told him—lying through my teeth of course, which made Tomy grimace openly—that I wanted a souvenir photo of him, the greatest mechanic in the world. Then we loaded up all of our luggage, including Chantal's large suitcase, and a gray briefcase with metal corners that she never let out of her sight.

We found out that it contained documents that even she didn't know the contents of, which she had to deliver to the French embassy in Ankara. We had enough trouble already and hoped fervently that no one decided to come after Chantal's gray briefcase as well. We had also, just to mention it, cleaned every surface and corner that we might come into to contact with using an acrid disinfectant: the radio, the glove compartment, and the handles on the doors. We didn't trust anyone anymore.

Our caution turned out to be unnecessary. During the long journey I told my companions everything that I had learnt about extraterrestrials over the years, or at least the fundamentals. Tomy already knew everything I knew up to my 22nd birthday or so; Marc had only read one of my books and Chantal knew next to nothing about my activities as a researcher. It was normal for me to be bombarded with questions and Chantal and Marc lived up to my expectations in that respect. Tomy, on the other hand, didn't interrupt me one single time. He simply listened in silence, an indefinable smile crossing his features every now and again. Agreement or rejection? Mockery or knowledge? It was impossible to tell. Shortly before we got to Ankara he asked, if I would agree to be taken over. It would be the simplest way for him to understand the way I thought, he explained. Of course, I agreed.

We reached Ankara in the early evening—unmolested. Chantal had had seven hours in the car to work her charms on Marc, and the two promptly disappeared into a double suite in the Sheraton. Tomy and I were given a suite with two rooms.

While Marc and Chantal were enjoying each other's company, Tomy took me over. And that was surely a far greater pleasure than what the two young lovers had ever experienced.

...AND THERE WAS LIGHT!

It was our last night in the Suvretta House Hotel and we had decided to give the alcohol a rest. Marc and I were sipping mineral water in the elegant dining room. In this room the tradition that the *chefs de rang* wore black and the trainees white still held sway. Their light steps made not the slightest noise as they crossed the light-blue wall-to-wall carpet. Candles flickered everywhere and chandeliers cast a subdued light down on the room. All that could be heard of the other guests was a muted murmur-murmur. The meals—the menu didn't change daily, but they were never the same twice—weren't simply carried out, but borne to your table by a whole team. It was a culinary celebration. In this restaurant dinner was a delight, a show, even. The whole thing was accompanied by gentle piano music, pleasant tunes from all over the world.

"Tomy took you over back there in the Sheraton in Ankara," Marc's voice was almost breathless with anticipation, "but you've never spoken about it. Come on, tell me what happened."

"I can't," I stated matter-of-factly.

"Can't, or won't?"

"Oh, I want to all right, but I can't really find the words."

"But you're an author! People like you have learnt how to describe stuff!"

I nodded. "That's true. But not the indescribable."

Marc's curiosity was too much for him to let the matter lie. He pressed and pressed, wheedled and begged and finally began to mock:

"Did you have sex with each other?" he asked.

"Ach! Rubbish!" I shot back at him. "I've never been gay and Tomy wasn't either." And then I relaxed and joked: "Or do you think I'd do it with my own brother? Come on!"

"Why are you being so secretive then? After all, Tomy took me over, too. I told you all about it," Marc said.

Thank God we hadn't drunk any alcohol. I started trying to sort out my memories of that evening, to transport myself back to that night in the Sheraton in Ankara, as Marc and Chantal had given in to their all-too-human instincts and Tomy and I had sat opposite each other in those heavy leather armchairs. Tomy had had that enigmatic smile on his lips as he asked me if I still wanted to go ahead with the takeover. When I nodded my assent, he said that it would be fine for me to stay sitting in my chair, but it would be better for him to lie down, so his body didn't tip over while he was out of it. What happened next was—in the true sense of the word—indescribable. And even though I attempted it, it was, at best, merely using the crutch of language, hollow words that could never come close to approaching those feelings; with a crippled understanding that seems wounded to me. I was attempting to put something into words that was so far beyond words, something that remains incomprehensible, even now though I constantly try to retrieve it from my memories. Normal reason is powerless to comprehend what happened to my consciousness while Tomy took me over.

"Picture this," I said to Marc. "You're on a quiz show and there are millions of people in the audience. And you have an unbelievable ability: you know everything that has ever been published in any book. The quizmaster hands you a thick book and asks you what is on page 421, in the second paragraph, and in the third line down. You're not allowed to open the book to see what's inside, but instead you press the book to your temples and answer: 'On page 421, second paragraph, the third line down reads: *As night finally fell, the tart poured herself her fourth whisky.*' The quote is exactly right: the audience goes wild. The quizmaster brings you another book: it's called *The Knowledge of the Ancient Chinese*. You have never seen or heard of this book in your whole life. This time he asks what is on page 114, third paragraph, first line. Again you hold the book to your temple, close your eyes and answer: *The night's astronomical bearing report was necessary to set the compass course*. On a big screen behind you the audience can see what really is on page 114 of the book. Your answer is exactly the same as what is on the page. The audience is ecstatic and the quizmaster nods appreciatively and asks you: 'That's unbelievable, absolutely incredible. How do you do it?' What, my dear Marc, is your answer?"

We looked at each other for a second or two. And then he said: "There is no such ability. But if I really could do it, I don't know what I'd answer."

"Exactly! That's something like the way I feel. What happened in my consciousness while Tomy took me over is just as inexplicable."

"Couldn't you try to explain it with images?" Marc insisted. "You must have seen something, even if it was just fragments of colors..."

"OK, Marc," I said to him, resigned to the fact that he wasn't going to give up until I at least made the attempt, "I'll try to illustrate how the whole thing went. But it'll only be a vague approximation. I didn't really 'see' anything—that's not really the right word for it. I didn't see anything with my eyes, because I had no eyes.

"Anyway, here goes. After Tomy had gone off to his room to lie down, I laid my arms on the broad armrests of the armchair, leant my head back and stared up at the ceiling light. I lifted my feet up to rest them on a low table in front of the chair and, in the process, knocked over a bottle of mineral water, which had been stood on the table. I went to bend down and catch it before the carpet got wet, but I never got that far. Suddenly I was light as a feather: I took off and flew up through the ceiling, through the concrete walls of the hotel. And at the same time, waves of contentment were flowing through me. A feeling that mere human emotions cannot describe. Not just exhilaration, more like a hurricane of elation. I raced through the universe and can actually remember calling out for Tomy, although I couldn't call anything as I had no body…"

"And?" interrupted Marc, "Did he answer?"

"Yes! He said to my spirit, or consciousness, or my energy form, or whatever it was, that I should just let go. And he laughed. I laughed, too. Just imagine, Marc, I laughed loudly and without a care in the world, and all this without any vocal chords, air, lungs or any of the things that we humans need to laugh. I was intoxicated and unbelievably happy, riding a rollercoaster that wasn't even there. My thoughts—if they were thoughts—told me that every earthly 3-D theater that I had ever visited and gazed in wonderment at, was ridiculously simple in comparison with this. I raced on—you'll hardly believe this, Marc—through suns without noticing the slightest hint of heat.

I burst through thunderous clouds of indescribable coldness, through oceans, and through the glutinous mouths of volcanoes. I saw beings that are beyond my power to explain; they looked back at me as I passed and I smelled smells that I shouldn't have even been able to smell without a nose. I shot through spaceships that were larger than cities, crafts that made those in Hollywood science fiction films look like children's toys. I experienced color combinations that couldn't exist. I saw myself as a hologram reproduced hundreds and thousands of times everywhere and at different ages—from a baby to an old man. I saw life forms and knew that they were me, although I couldn't understand how that could be—but somehow I *could* understand, nevertheless. Just imagine an arachnoid being that stares at you with huge eyes and you suddenly sense a tremendous wave of wellbeing, and then you realize that you are looking at yourself.

"Then everything was quiet and all movement stopped. I could sense the ticking of a clock and found myself standing in the biggest library you could ever imagine. Books as far as the eye could see, in every direction: above me, below me, to my left and right. I turned my nonexistent head and understood that I knew everything that was in all these books. And I knew, too, *how* I knew everything: it was because all of these works were written by universal beings and that I myself was one of these beings and everything is linked and interwoven in a wondrous way.

"I dived into subatomic space: neutrons, protons and electrons whizzed and whirred around me. And then a kind of ripple ran through this miniature solar system and the particles shifted their position, the atom changing into a completely new one. All of this took place at an unimaginable pace and yet at the same time in slow motion. The electrons sprang so quickly from one atom to another that a kind of universe of oscillations or vibrations came into being where the electrons spread their eternal message. I felt the need to understand it, and I did understand it for a second as I was sucked into an electron, like falling into a black hole. Inside, I found myself suddenly back in the library with the billions of books. Marc, I thought I could hear organ music, then jazz, Bach, Gregorian chants, *All You Need Is Love* by the Beatles, the long-dead drummer Gene Krupa, Louis Armstrong, Mozart, Frédéric Chopin's Piano Concerto No.1, the *Bolero* by Ravel ... the list goes on and on... and then I was spat back out of the electron into a new universe with new atomic nuclei and electrons in other solar systems, which I quietly understood, astonished and deeply moved at the same time, were—because of the multitudes of suns, planets, and colors—different to the other atomic models.

Then whole star systems started moving towards a pitch-black abyss, what we would call a black hole, with me in the middle of it all. Time stood still. Everything, every speck of material in the star system, including me, solidified as if it had crystallized until a mighty current spewed everything out the other side. What had been solar systems were now microscopic beads that began to glow whiter than white, then expanded, and finally exploded. I understood that all the solar systems that were consumed by black holes were spat out at another place and time in a kind of new big bang. Marc, there isn't just one 'Big Bang' that led to the creation of the universe, like we learn in school, but millions of the things that are going off constantly somewhere in the space-time continuum. Galaxies come and go like CO_2 bubbles in a bath full of mineral water.

"During this crazy train ride I started feeling a kind of not unpleasant pressure, and I wanted to return

144

to Earth, to my body. I felt a strong breeze, although I was hanging in empty space and, what's more, had no body to feel it with. Galaxies and star systems flew by me, stretching into blazing lines of light. They swelled into bright points of luminosity, fused together, flew apart, crashed into each other, and shot off in different directions. I dived into this iridescent lightshow of vibrations, the oscillations between atomic nuclei and electrons. Suddenly, I recognized our solar system, with ringed Saturn and mighty Jupiter. I flew straight through the glowing ball of our sun and off towards Earth, towards Ankara, back through the concrete walls of the hotel and then I opened my eyes. My pulse was normal; my feet were still propped on the small table; I heard the whirr of the air-conditioning and noticed the bottle of mineral water on the floor.

Taken aback, I realized that only a few drops of water were gone: the water was still flowing out of the bottle. I picked it up and stared up at the ceiling. A warm feeling of immense gratitude spread through me. I understood that I had experienced the universe and at the same time I realized how insignificantly microscopic I was. Never before in my life—and never since—have I felt so powerful and yet, at the same time, so small."

Marc had lit a cigarette and stared at me in silence. After a while he spoke:

"And now you're back?"

"Of course! Just as you know and love me!" I said with a wink. "I suppose you think I'm crazy."

"Not at all, not at all. A fraction of what you described happened to me, too, when Tomy took me over. And afterwards? What happened then?"

"I had placed the bottle of mineral water back on the table and wanted to sit back and contemplate the grandiose vision I had just had when Tomy appeared and plunked himself down in the armchair next to me.

He was wearing his Mona Lisa smile again. He nodded his head and stretched out his right hand toward me. Then he enquired good-naturedly if I was feeling all right. I nodded and stammered something like: 'Yes, little, big brother' and 'Thank you! Thank you!' I was overloaded and overwhelmed. I stared at Tomy's face for several minutes. It was still a great effort for me to understand that behind this youthful face, this young human body, the fragile piece of flesh and bone, these dark eyes and enigmatic smile was a being of universal energy. At some stage I asked him how long the whole thing had lasted. He pointed at the bottle of mineral water and said: "Time enough for three gulps of water to flow out."

"I know it's all true," said Marc quietly, "but no one's ever gonna buy that story."

"It doesn't matter," I told him. "I know what I know and the privilege of having seen this wondrous vision is enough for me. I asked Tomy if experiencing this universal show would have any lasting effect on me and he revealed to me that in the future I would be able to write my books with far greater ease than ever before. I would just have to concentrate inwardly and the sources and quotes would just come to me, as if whispered into my ear by ghostly voices. And he told me something else that confused me more than it made anything clearer. He explained that all the people about whom I had really strong feelings, such as love, but also those who I really hated, had been with me in earlier lives. Every life form possesses its own distinctive nucleus that moves on from one life to the next. I should nurture the love and try and eradicate the hate. I should pray for all those people who have done me harm and ask the great spirit of the universe to forgive them for their deeds. Even after their deaths."

"And that's going to help them?" asked Marc.

"Apparently not just them, but us, too, in the next round. And because I believe everything that Tomy told me, that must mean that you and I, Marc, must have known each other in an earlier existence. And Elisabeth and I, too. And all the others, who I love or hate. Tomy also explained that I should try to see the universe as a kind of convoluted hologram. Everything is connected to everything else, and time only exists for the material objects and the vibrations that arise from them."

**

Our farewell dinner in St. Moritz was supposed to have been a sober affair, but I was so churned up inside that my body was yearning for a good red wine. The wine waiter brought us a bottle of *Château Mouton Rothschild*. He handed me the cork to sniff and decanted the heavy wine in the flickering candlelight. While I watched the burgundy-colored liquid slowly pouring into the fat-bellied decanter, it seemed to me as if a Milky Way of millions of tiny glittering stars were flowing through the air. We toasted each other, smiling. Marc asked me if Tomy had ventured any opinion regarding my theories about extraterrestrials.

"Not that evening in Ankara. We didn't get round to discussing the subject. But we did later."

"And?"

"Tomy went much further than I ever have. As I told you on the trip to Ankara in the car, I'm convinced that the Earth was visited at least twice in ancient times by extraterrestrials. But Tomy spoke of 16 visits over the last 500,000 years. The other 14 visits are way too far back in time. But—and this'll blow your mind, Marc—Tomy told me that the definitive proof for the alien visits lies in our genes!"

Marc pulled a face and tilted his head a little to one side: "What's that supposed to mean?"

"If you had read my books, you'd know that I have always maintained that mankind is not solely a product of evolution. We have evolved, yes, but at some stage in our development a specific, artificial genetic mutation was introduced—and that was provided by the extraterrestrials that manipulated the primitive hominids that were our forefathers. Our mythology is full of reports about this intervention—it's all in my books. Even the Bible reports that God made man in his own image. So far, so good. Tomy went on to say that we would be able to identify this intervention in our genes: our genes also contain a message from the extraterrestrials that is clear as day and cannot be refuted. We only have to find the message."

"Great! Can we do that?"

"At the moment, our geneticists are not advanced enough, but in around 25 years—so Tomy reckons—the message should be revealed."

"That would be around 2012. Are you still going to be around for that?"

"I hope so! And then we can start with the next big debate, because the proof of alien intervention will throw a whole new light on our religions. *Capito*?"

Marc nodded quietly. He didn't really understand much about evolution or genetics. He was far more interested in what Tomy had said. I interrupted his thoughts with a completely unrelated question.

"You spent two nights with Chantal in Ankara," I said. "Then you turned up, sour-faced, dragging your stuff into our suite. What happened?"

Marc seemed to find the subject embarrassing. He gulped down his wine quickly, choking in the process. Then he admitted that he had wanted to tell me the story for some time, but had not been able to get me alone.

Chantal, so he explained, was very experienced—sexually. She did things with him that he had never dreamed of. The next day she had been collected by a limousine from the French embassy—along with her metal-cornered briefcase. She had stayed there the whole afternoon and she didn't return until early evening. That night she had driven him once more to the pinnacles of lust and then during the post-coital cigarette started saying outrageous things about Tomy: he was a monster, didn't belong on Earth; he was dangerous and would bring down our entire society. She said that Tomy's body wasn't a real body, not born but constructed artificially, a dung pile of chemicals. This object needed to be got rid of, before something awful happened. Marc, too, had a responsibility towards humanity: killing Tomy wouldn't be murder because Tomy wasn't human. He would be doing his duty to mankind.

Marc looked over to me with a sad expression on his face. "Do you understand? I couldn't listen to her talk anymore. After the sex, it was like she was a different person. She was like a whore and I was the dumb fool she was using to get her way. Maybe they'd spent the whole afternoon in the embassy turning her inside out; I don't know what got into her. I was so furious, I almost hit her. So I just grabbed my bag, threw my washing things into it and came and knocked on your door. You know the rest."

Indeed I did. Although I wouldn't have described what followed next in this impossible story as 'the rest.' The chaos was just beginning.

THE HOLOGRAPHIC UNIVERSE

My plan on the day after we arrived in Ankara was to get rid of the Range Rover and to send my companions back to Switzerland—separately. The most important thing was to avoid remaining in any grouping that made us easy to identify; anything which would make us show up on their computers. So the Rover had to go. Its coloration and Swiss license plate made it unmistakable and it would be immediately associated with our group.

The previous night, the night after my amazing journey through the universe, Marc had turned up in our suite. He didn't say a thing and it didn't look like anything we could say would restore him to words, so we didn't even try. He just threw himself down onto the double bed next to Tomy. Something unpleasant must have happened between him and Chantal. So it made it all the more easy to part with her the next day. She booked a flight to Paris—Marc didn't even shake her hand. He simply turned away without a word. To me she said: "We'll be seeing one another." And to Tomy: "You and I in particular."

"What did she mean?" I asked him when she was gone. "Don't ask me. I can't make head nor tail of the woman.

One of these days—whether I want to or not—I'm going to have to get to the bottom of all this."

The receptionist in the hotel helped me to contact an international customs agent who helped me to arrange transport to Venice for the Rover. He photocopied my passport and took receipt of the *carnet de passage*, the car's passport. It cost me twelve hundred dollars and I would be able to collect my vehicle from the duty-free harbor in Venice in 12 days' time. In the offices of American Express I collected some more cash and asked about flights to Italy, Austria and Holland. That, in itself, was no problem—except for Marc and Tomy. They didn't want to be separated, at any cost, and insisted on staying together. Again, I thought about the friendship poem by Schiller that had come back to me in the desert of Baluchistan and which I had recited to Marc to distract him from his thirst: "Tis mine your suppliant now to be, Ah, let the band of love—be three!"

In the foyer of the Sheraton I discovered a prospectus for the Orient Express. A light went on in my head. That was the answer! I had read somewhere or other that the old Orient Express, immortalized by Agatha Christie in her world-famous novel *Murder on the Orient Express*, had been revived by a new company. A luxury train with a stylishly decorated dining car, a piano bar, and immaculate sleeping cabins. My companions were equally enthusiastic when I told them about my idea. They both clapped their hands in delight. Just to throw the bloodhounds off the trail, I booked a flight for Tomy from Ankara to Athens—

which he would never use, of course—and one for Marc from Ankara to Zürich. Money thrown out the window for the sake of our own personal safety.

The next day we rented a car, a brand new Opel, and set off to cover the 370 kilometers to Istanbul. The highway was relatively new and in very good condition, which was good, because I had no intention of stopping anywhere along the way and especially not spending another night in a hotel where we would have to use our passports to register. Luckily, I knew a reliable travel agent in Istanbul, which I had used on earlier visits.

"The next journey on the Orient Express?" smiled the plump lady with the round face. "The train arrived this morning and is due to leave at 17:04 headed for Thessaloniki and Athens. You require a three-bed cabin? That will be difficult, sir. That combination is usually booked up."

"But, Madame," I insisted, "we're traveling all the way to Switzerland!"

She managed to find us a cabin and I asked innocently—whereupon Tomy walked out shaking his head—if she could reserve the cabin under the name Baumgartner.

"But you are well-known here, Mr. von Däniken!"

Precisely for that reason, I lied. We wanted to travel incognito, I continued, without being molested by obtrusive fans. The manager of the travel agent, a charming Turk with the (how could it be any different?) obligatory mustache arrived and explained that when we came to customs we would have to show our travel documents and fill in our real names anyway.

"Of course," I assured him. "All that's important to me is that I can book the cabin under the name Baumgartner. Then I need a written confirmation from the travel agency that we three can use Mr. Baumgartner's cabin because he had to cancel at the last minute. Naturally, I will recompense you for your troubles."

After this I counted out 300 dollars onto the desk. A hundred dollars extra for each of us, I thought, this was going to be the most expensive trip that I ever take on the Orient Express. As it turned out, it's the only one I've ever taken.

As I was convinced that there was no level to which the secret police wouldn't stoop in terms of dirty tricks, we agreed to all board the train separately. I suggest to my friends that they try out a small restaurant that I had once visited with Ercan on the banks of the Bosporus. I took myself off in another direction, strolling through one of the many bazaars, arriving on the platform just a few minutes before the train was due to depart. Tomy and Marc were already waiting for me in our cabin.

I immediately pulled the curtain closed and the train slowly pulled out of the station, steaming along the Bosporus past the Topkapi Palace and the ancient city wall. It made its way through the Istanbul suburbs before leaving the city behind it and in less than two hours we were at the border crossing at Ipsala. Twice I was filled with anxiety: the first time when the Turkish border police came and checked our passports and then again as the Greek police did the same a short while later. Then the train clattered on its way once more. As we saw the city sign for Ferrai we all hugged each other in relief: we were finally in Greece!

The journey to Switzerland took several days, but nothing happened to arouse our suspicions. Every night before we went to bed we stuck adhesive tape over the keyhole and along the bottom of the door. In this amateur manner we intended to hinder any attempts to spray poison into the cabin, but fortunately nothing happened. Either the "service" was waiting for a better opportunity, or they really had lost sight of us. Our conversations during the journey inevitably turned to the subject of Tomy. How were we going to introduce him? I expected no great problems with Elisabeth: she would catch on quickly and play along. But what about my brothers and sisters? They knew, after all, that I didn't have any illegitimate brother, especially from our long-dead father. How would I explain Tomy in the office?

Marc didn't take it so seriously and laughed: "Ha! Just imagine, you turn up with a guy who looks just like you, only a lot younger and better looking!"

Tomy announced in a matter-of-fact way that he wasn't planning on being a burden to us for long. He still wanted to visit a few people and all he needed was a safe place to lie down while he did it.

"Who do you want to visit?" asked Marc, genuinely interested.

"I'm thinking of scientists, maybe one or the other religious leader, maybe even one of your most hypocritical species: the politician. Although a couple of those should be plenty…"

I interrupted him.

"I don't understand," I said. "You already comprehend everything. You know the universe and all its interconnections, which I also got to see, thanks to you…"

It didn't sound too cheery.

"Not so fast, big brother," Tomy broke in. "I still don't know how mankind thinks; what makes humans tick; why they are the way they are. But I don't believe in forcing anyone to do anything against their wills: I will ask for permission first."

"You'll only be disappointed!" I said darkly, "My fellow humans are generally egocentric, self-opinionated, know-it-alls, and—as you already suspect—a bunch of liars. I can't imagine how that could benefit your home world."

"You didn't turn out so bad," Tomy grinned at me. "Your opinions and your specialist knowledge will enrich my society. Just imagine a computer that has stored enormous amounts of knowledge and has also developed its own emotions. But the computer isn't omniscient. Every new piece of knowledge is precious to it, because it brings the computer more opportunities for exchanging ideas, thoughts, and concepts. It makes it, so to speak, wiser and more knowledgeable."

I had an idea of what he meant, so I said nothing.

***

We disembarked from the Orient Express in Lausanne, an old city clinging to the mountainside on the banks of Lake Geneva, and took a Swiss train. I called Elisabeth. She was overjoyed to hear that we had got back safely and offered to cook Marc and me a special meal that evening.

"Not tonight, my dear," I insisted. "We should go out to eat: I want to be alone with you. And bring your car, will you? Mine is still on a cruise!"

She knew me well enough not to ask too many questions.

As soon as the train reached Solothurn, we took a taxi to the Hotel Krone. The Krone, as the locals call it was situated in the center of the medieval baroque town. At some point in history Napoleon is said to have stopped the night in the hotel. I booked a single room for Tomy and asked him to wait in his room until I called for him. Marc was picked up by his mother, who hugged and kissed him in floods of tears of joy and thanked me countless times for bringing him back safely.

Alone at last, I wandered over to a quiet table in the corner of the restaurant and waited tensely for Elisabeth. I had to introduce her to Tomy, but as gently as possible. I thought about her as I sat there. She was a good woman. Kishon might have said: "The best wife of all." I met her in a small tearoom in Zürich in an age when jukeboxes still reigned. Back then, in 1959, I was always putting on records by Frank Sinatra or Dean Martin and Elisabeth aroused my curiosity by choosing a song called "Chanson d'amour." The whole bar roared out the refrain, now well known all around the world: "Ra-ta-ta-ta- da!" Elisabeth was from a town in North Rhine-Westphalia in Germany and was doing an apprenticeship in a bar in Zürich. Her parents in faraway Westphalia ran a small farm and I admired them both.

People of few words, generous and industrious, they were. At that time, I was working as a waiter in a five-star hotel and the tearoom where I met Elisabeth was the favorite hangout for me and my group of friends. The love between Elisabeth and I blossomed very quickly and we soon decided to marry. That happened on July 20, 1960. That was 27 years ago, and I have often wondered since then if she would have married me if she had known what she was letting herself in for. How many waiters end up as controversial writers? Elisabeth—who I soon started calling Ebet—remained a rock and helped me through all the ups and downs of my career with stoical patience. But now she would have a real test of her character, I thought. And I had to explain a second Erich, who was thirty years younger!

After she had greeted each "me," drank an aperitif and asked the usual questions, she looked me straight in the eyes and asked, "OK, Erich, what's bothering you? Why the cloak and dagger routine?"

"Oh, Ebet!" I began, "I really do have a quite

unique problem! Something which happened to me in the desert of Baluchistan and I don't know quite how to tell you about it…"

"Did you get an Arab girl into trouble?" she interrupted, her eyes glinting dangerously.

"Heavens, no! What are you thinking? No, my problem has nothing to do with sex; rather it's a young man. A 22-year-old man, to be precise."

Now Ebet looked at me extremely skeptically. Yet I could feel her relief that my problem had nothing to do with infidelity.

"Have you adopted someone?" she asked.

"Ebet, really!" I said. "How on earth would I end up adopting anybody in the middle of a desert? What would I want with a 22-year-old Arab?"

"I know you, Erich, with your compassion! But now stop beating around the bush and tell me whatever it is you want to tell me!"

"Please, Ebet. Don't interrupt and you will understand everything."

I slowly told her the story of what had happened, leaving nothing out. About how Tomy came into being, his work with the Iranian secret service, the sabotage on our Range Rover on Nemrut Daği, Ercan's death in the underground city and even our trip on the Orient Express.

At the end of my description, she remarked dryly: "A good story; it would make a great novel. But you could have told me all this at home."

"Ebet!" I pleaded and held out my hand. "Tomy is *here*, two floors up; above this very restaurant!"

"Then show me this wonder boy!"

I took the elevator up to the second floor, told Tomy what he had to do, and returned with him to Elisabeth who remained waiting at our table. She looked up just as we were approaching and her spoon, which she had just loaded with mousse au *chocolat*, clattered from her hand to the floor. She held on fast to the edge of the table with both hands, as if she were afraid that she might fall otherwise. And then we were standing next to her. She took a deep breath and looked closely at Tomy. He stood there, like a well-behaved schoolboy, with his hands clasped behind his back.

"Erich?" she murmured questioningly, and then twice more, drawn out, "Erich? Erich?"

Tomy smiled my sweetest smile from thirty years ago. He exuded an overpowering charm. Elisabeth rubbed her sweating palms on the white tablecloth and Tomy, clearly master of this situation, held out his hand to her:

"Grüezi," he said, using the traditional Swiss greeting. "I'm sorry if I startled you or upset you in any way. But this is the only body I have. Your husband kindly gave me the name Tomy."

Ebet said nothing for the moment and tried to catch her breath. Then Tomy held out his left hand, too, pointing to the mole on the back of his hand.

"I'm genuine, see? Erich must have told you how I came into being."

I grabbed a chair from a neighboring table and pressed Tomy gently into it. Elisabeth grabbed hold of Tomy's left hand and began stroking it gently. She stared constantly into his eyes. Then she took his right hand as well and pressed it firmly. Then I knew: she had dealt with the shock.

"Tomy, welcome to our world," were her first words and then—typical Elisabeth—she jested, "But how am I supposed to tell which one of you is my husband? Erich could have traveled through time. He is friends with the strangest people: maybe one of them sent him into the past. And maybe you, Tomy, are really my Erich, while he," she pointed playfully at

159

me, "doesn't really exist at all. What are we going to do with the old fellow?"

The two of them laughed loudly at this uproarious humor: I stood speechless to one side.

Later, Ebet insisted that Tomy should come and live with us. He couldn't stay here in the hotel, she said, it would just lead to too many complications. We would make up a guest room for him and, for the time being at least, would introduce him to nobody. Except for our very closest friends and even then only after carefully preparing the ground beforehand. Back then—1987, as you recall—the American TV series *Alf* was extremely popular.

This situation strongly reminded me of Alf, a strange-looking beast that had somehow made its way from space to our planet and ended up living with a stereotypical American family, learning English very quickly in the process. But Alf couldn't be shown to the neighbors, let alone the rest of humanity. Alf, a hilarious TV show, stretched the bounds of reality. Alf was a fictional character—Tomy was real. We talked about it, laughed about it, too.

But Tomy assured us that he was grateful just to be allowed to live in just one room and maybe occasionally stroll around the garden. He didn't need to travel and he certainly wouldn't be a burden on us for long.

Elisabeth's answer to this was that he could stay for the rest of his life if he wanted: he would certainly never be a burden for us. She really seemed to enjoy Tomy's company and if I hadn't known that Tomy— after his one and only sexual encounter with Chantal— felt no desire for physical relationships, I might have even been jealous. So we packed everything into the car and drove on to Feldbrunnen on the outskirts of Solothurn. The house where we lived was a roomy three-story villa with a small park and a large meadow behind the house.

It was shortly before midnight when we arrived home. Ebet reached for her keys and let us in quickly as a biting wind was chilling us to the bone. Inside the house, our three dogs barked loudly: a small white Highland Terrier, a black Tibetan Highland Mastiff and our imposing Great Dane who—when she laid her great paws on my shoulders—was much bigger than me. A fabulous, friendly, giant beast that put the wind up practically every stranger to visit the house. All three dogs protected my wife jealously; what would they make of Tomy?

The house door was barely open a crack before Neptune, the Great Dane, was out greeting Elisabeth enthusiastically and leaping up and licking my face and wagging his tail like a loon; he ended up doing exactly the same with Tomy as if he had always been a part of the family. Even the little white Terrier bounced excitedly around us all. Only the Tibetan Mastiff, who never liked being stroked anyway, kept its emotions in check.

Finally lying in my own bed, I was looking forward to a good, long, peaceful sleep. But the next morning at seven o'clock everything was no longer all right with the world. A long, high-pitched scream split the air, accompanied by the clatter of falling crockery. I ran downstairs, still clad in my pajamas. There stood our 19-year-old housemaid, Edith, as if glued to the spot, a tray of broken plates and saucers on the floor beside her. Two meters away stood Tomy, dressed only in his underpants. Edith's face was distorted with fear and when she saw me her knees finally gave way and she sank, deathly pale, to the floor in a faint.

By now Elisabeth was also on the scene. We carried Edith into her room. Ebet fetched some cold wet cloths and a bottle of some foul-reeking substance that she held under Edith's nose. Tomy disappeared into his room to put on some clothes. Elisabeth sat down on the edge of the bed and spoke gently to the traumatized girl. When Edith had finally calmed down a little, my wife explained that the strange man who had frightened her so very much was, in fact, my youngest brother. My father had only been twenty when I was born and thirty years later Tomy had been a bit of a surprise. Thank heavens Tomy wasn't around to hear this white lie!

As soon as Edith felt up to it, we invited Tomy to come into the room. He behaved like an enchanting young prince, begged forgiveness for his unexpected appearance, and scolded us that we hadn't warned him that we had such a delightful young lady in our service. This was true. We had simply forgotten to mention it. Elisabeth went red with embarrassment, but I already saw the next problem looming on the horizon of human emotions. At breakfast, which I normally do without, Elisabeth informed us that Neptune, the Great Dane, who for years had slept by her door, had now found a new resting place in front of Tomy's room. Even now he was lying at Tomy's feet.

It would have been a waste of time taking Tomy around the large house to show him all the different rooms: my library, the archive with its 80,000 slides, the correspondence from readers, the four bathrooms in the villa, the garden. Since that wondrous night in the Sheraton when Tomy had taken me over he knew everything that I knew.

And now he moved around the house as if he had lived there all his life. And he cooked just like me, too! That evening he cooked—much to my wife's amazement—spaghetti bolognaise exactly the way I always prepare it. Even the salad sauce, my unique creation, was no secret to him as if he ate it every day back on his home planet.

Whenever Edith was present, we avoided talking about Tomy's origin or special talents. We didn't want her to find out who Tomy really was: Tomy agreed, and although he couldn't lie, he would simply say nothing on the subject. Then he asked us if we could lock him in his room: he wanted to remain undisturbed during his 'travels.' Elisabeth didn't think that that was such a good idea, but instead looked around and found one of those 'Do not disturb' signs that you get in hotels. She said she would tell Edith not to go in whenever the sign was hanging on the door. It wasn't a good idea to lock him in, she said, because if he needed to get out of his room, for whatever reason, and neither of us was around, he would be trapped.

"Just imagine: what if the house was on fire?" Annoyingly, Tomy's door wouldn't let itself be locked from the inside—the lock was from the 18th century and showed no inclination of changing its mind—so we were left with the sign as the only option. Tomy shook his head and glanced up at me. We knew that nothing would happen to him.

The Villa Serdang, where we were living, was right on the main road from Solothurn towards Olten. Every day, thousands of cars drove by—in both directions. In addition, there were a set of rails embedded in the asphalt on which "the Green Lisa"—as we called our local train—rattled by the house every half hour or so. The noise wasn't actually that bad as we were separated from the road by a thick stone wall and the 18th century villa had very solid walls.

Next to the villa was a small park containing a few trees and a small pond, home to a colony of frogs. Behind the house, there was a meadow as large as a football field. The ground floor of the villa included the kitchen, a toilet, the well-lit conservatory with its large glass windows, and two living rooms with high stucco ceilings. One of these rooms contained my library, a book collection featuring all of the mysteries of this world plus reference works on space travel, genetics, and religious philosophy. We used the second room as a living room—it was equipped with upholstered armchairs, a television, and an open fireplace that was so big you could roast a piglet in it. Upstairs, there were several bedrooms and bathrooms: the whole house consisted of 26 rooms, but we didn't use all of them. The other part of the house was lived in by my sister Leni and her family. Unlike TV families, who are constantly plagued by arguments and feuds, the von Däniken household was very harmonious.

It was obvious to Elisabeth and me that we were going to have to introduce Tomy to Leni and her two children sooner or later. How were we going to explain Tomy? We discussed the problem at length. Tomy, as usual, would not accept any solution, which did not consist of the whole truth and assured us that when he met my sister he would tell her everything.

Man proposes and God disposes, I thought, when it finally did happen. Leni had a key for our half of the house so she could bring her dogs through the house and exercise them on the meadow. Because it was Edith's night off, Tomy was helping us by clearing up in the kitchen after dinner when Leni suddenly walked in to fetch the dogs' collars from the hook where they always hang. Tomy and Leni managed to walk right into each other. With great presence of mind, Tomy said: "Excuse me, I'll just go and get Erich." Leni plunked herself down onto the nearest stool in stunned amazement.

She looked extremely confused and her face was extremely pale as I came in. Valiantly, she pressed her lips together and managed a wan smile. Leni, you need to know, is my oldest sister. She has a generous and warm character, and she cooks better than any top chef in the world. Her husband, a high-ranking police officer, had died a few months earlier and her two grown-up children had moved out. Really, Leni deserved a bit of peace in her old age -time to relax, to go to concerts, or to just be alone. But all the family business and her friends kept her on her toes. Now she was sat on the stool, nervously wringing the dog leashes in her hands.

"Erich, who is this man?" she asked. "Tell me, who *is* he?"

I sat down next to her and Ebet came over and joined us. I answered her straight: it was a long story, but she needn't worry, it had nothing to do with sex, illicit behavior or anything illegal, more to do with the kind of things my books were about. This was pretty much the truth. Hesitantly and somewhat unsure about everything, Leni followed us into the living room. Tomy stood up, courteously and offered his hand, which she took with a sigh. Then we uncorked one of America's best red wines, an Opus One from the vineyards of Robert Mondavi.

Robert—his friends call him Bob—and I had met several years ago in Acapulco. I had been the guest speaker at a seminar given by a U.S. oil company. Managers from various different professional walks of life were invited to give talks about their diverse specialties. Bob and I were among them. At the bar, he had explained to me that the majority of his countrymen knew little of wine. Even when tucking into a fine prime rib of beef, they would rather drink water. I could confirm that from my own experiences in the restaurant trade. Back in the 60s I had been appalled by American table manners. They would hardly have sat down at their tables, before they started munching bread and gulping down water.

I had endured the traumatic experience of watching Americans enjoy our national dish, the cheese fondue, while slurping down hot chocolate! Awful! Bob Mondavi—whose wife is Swiss, by the way—was complaining back then about his father who owned a huge vineyard in California which only mass-produced second-rate wine. Until Bob met up with the Frenchman Baron Philippe de Rothschild, that is. The Rothschilds ran one of world's most famous vineyards in Bordeaux, which had been producing fine quality wines for decades. Bob Mondavi and Baron Philippe de Rothschild became firm friends. Together they managed to create a phenomenal wine by combining the years of knowledge and experience of the Rothschilds with an originally French grape, now ripened to perfection under the Californian sun. The wine was called Cabernet Sauvignon Opus One—a fine drop that is only served on very special occasions. The label displays, to this day, only the profiles of the two wine growers and their signatures. Back in Acapulco, Bob had presented me with an entire case of Opus One.

My sister Leni is one of those select few, who really know something about red wines. She watched appreciatively as I brought out the bottle, but her gaze flicked constantly back to Tomy as I poured out four glasses of the precious drink. Licking my lips in anticipation, I swilled the wine around in its bulbous crystal wine glass. The open fire and a few lighted candles enhanced a tranquil and yet tense atmosphere. It ended up being a long night. At the end of it, four bottles of Opus One stood empty on the mantelpiece. Leni had interrupted my story infrequently with short questions, such as: "Is there such a thing?" "How is that possible?" and "Did you really go through all that?"

Leni knew Marc from his frequent visits to Villa Serdang with his mother. "Marc was there from the very beginning!" I insisted, "Call him, if you don't believe me!"

In view of Tomy's presence, calling Marc wasn't really necessary. Leni slowly became accustomed to seeing him there, and even attempted to joke around with him a little. She still repeatedly stared at him in amazement, though, grasping his hands and even stroking his hair.

"I knew you as a lad, Erich. We grew up together..." Leni didn't know if she should look at me or Tomy. "Seeing you again like this is some kind of miracle! The voice, those buckteeth—it's all exactly like it was thirty years ago. Unbelievable!"

"What do you think I went through?" said Ebet wryly to her. "And still do, when I look at this handsome young fellow, smell him or hear him talking exactly like my husband from thirty years in the past!"

Then the two women raised the subject that I had put to the back of my mind: We shouldn't be so naïve as to think that the secret services would ever leave us alone. Did we think that the Turks would just forget Ercan's murder? That the Iranians would simply put Tomy's amazing abilities out of their minds?

"Don't think this is all over." Leni reaffirmed. "It's a shame my husband is gone," she said sadly, "he could have made contact with the Swiss secret services."

I hadn't even realized that we had a Swiss secret service. But even so, what could they have done for us? They would have just laughed at our story.

"But Tomy is here!" she said excitedly, Elisabeth nodding in support. "You could present the living proof that you're not lying: two Erich von Dänikens right next to each other. One old and one young. That's pretty hard evidence to refute!"

Tomy didn't think much of the idea of having to reveal his existence to any kind of ominous public servants. And what's more he didn't plan on staying for that long anyway. He would not be leaving the house, he insisted. The ladies sighed in resignation about so much male stubbornness.

The next morning brought the next episode. It seemed as though it was impossible to get a good night's sleep in my house these days. Banging loudly and impatiently on my door, Edith roused me from my slumbers. Luckily, the Opus One is such a good wine that my head remained clear.

"Come quickly, Mr. von Däniken, I think your younger brother is dead!" she cried in a high-pitched voice, barely managing to keep back her tears.

I ran down the stairs. Tomy's room was open: Neptune lay next to his bed. We had forgotten to hang up the 'Do not disturb' sign on the door! As I bent over Tomy to check his breathing and pulse, Neptune lifted his hulking head and began to growl. "It's all right, lad," I assured him. Tomy was breathing very shallowly, but regularly, his pulse was also OK. I covered him up with a blanket and went to reassure Edith. My brother was subject to epileptic fits, I lied and hoped that she didn't know anything about epilepsy. Then I hung the 'Do not disturb' sign from the door handle and admonished Edith not to bother my ailing brother. She nodded dutifully, but I had the feeling she didn't believe a word I was saying. I tried several tricks to try and tempt Neptune away from Tomy's bedside, but in vain. If I left him in there he would just open the door from the inside with his paws—a trick he had learnt when just a puppy. And if I tried to force him to lie outside the door, he would probably just open it and go back in again. So I decided to just leave him where he was and informed Ebet.

"Leave him be," she instructed me. "After all, what do we know about how dogs tick? Neptune knows why he's decided to protect Tomy—even if we don't."

Reluctantly, because it was still too early for me, I showered, dressed, and started going through the piles of correspondence that my secretary had laid on my desk during my absence.

It's unbelievable what complete strangers will ask of me: "Mr. von Däniken, how did it all start?" (It started when I was at school), "Have you ever seen a UFO?" (No), "Do you   believe in God?" (Yes), "Could you, perhaps, do a lecture for us, free of charge of course, it will be good publicity for you!" (Don't need it, thank you), or variation number two: "We will donate your fee to a charitable organization." (I decide what happens with my money, if you please), "I would like to draw up your horoscope. Where exactly where you born?" (In Zofingen!), "How do you finance your research?" (With my books and lectures), "Are you a freemason?" (No!), "I know everything about the pyramids. We could produce a book together!" (Oh, really?), "I need to speak to you immediately!" (Don't they all?), and so on, and so on. From the time my first book was published in March 1968 to the middle of 1987 I had received somewhere in the region of 8000 such letters.

I scribbled a few handwritten observations on the letters for my secretary. Thank God my office was in another building, or we would have never have gotten away with this game of hide-and-seek. My secretary had made several attempts to lure me into the office— she must have found out from Ebet that I was back. I wriggled out of it by telling her I had come back to Switzerland a few days earlier than planned because I needed the rest.

Suddenly Tomy appeared behind me, peering over my shoulder; Neptune was close behind him, wagging his tail happily.

"Any more unpleasant encounters?" I inquired.

Tomy shrugged his shoulders. "More interesting than unpleasant, I would say. The two people that allowed me into their minds were wonderful and,"—he laughed—"only one of them lied."

"Is there such a thing on Earth?" I asked.

"As I learnt, yes."

"Can you reveal any more?"

Tomy told me that he had been in the mind of a rich Swiss gentleman who had sweated profusely from fear during the takeover, but had then opened up and treated the whole experience as some kind of crazy adventure. The man was intelligent and adaptable. He had played along and the questions and answers had flown back and forth like a ball in a tennis match. It had been fun for both of them and now Tomy felt he understood the global finance system.

"Usually, these high-finance types are no angels," I interjected, "and they lie like there's no tomorrow. What was he called?"

Tomy told me the name, which I won't reveal here, and insisted that Mr. X had inherited much of his fortune and built it up using morally acceptable methods. He used his riches to support schools and orphanages, as well as scientific research in the field of biology. He had an insatiable appetite for knowledge and for that reason he had categorized Tomy's visit as a scientific phenomenon. "What's more, Mr. X considers your capitalist system to be completely corrupt."

"I am hearing you right? A rich capitalist who disapproves of capitalism? Why's he playing the game then?"

"Because at the moment—so I found out—no other system works. Mr. X believes in a worldwide currency, but doesn't think he will live to see it. Maybe he will call you."

"What!" I yelped in shock.

"Since my visit, Mr. X knows who you are and where I am staying. It would only be human, if he were to try and contact you."

Tomy pulled up a chair and sat down next to me. He explained that everyone that allowed him to take them over would know about me afterwards. It was unavoidable, he claimed, because they asked many questions and he was incapable of lying. And later, when Tomy was no longer among us, I did indeed receive letters from people who Tomy had "inhabited." There were even a few friendships that started that way. All of them kept the secret of Tomy to themselves otherwise—although a few of them only from a sense of self- protection. And not one of them ever lied to me, or me to them.

The second person that Tomy had taken over that morning was a high-ranking church dignitary in Germany. Grinning, Tomy told how the churchman had been afraid at first that the devil had possessed him. It had required a great deal of effort to persuade him otherwise and to calm him down enough to start a civilized dialog.

"Will he call me too?"

"I doubt it," said Tomy shaking his head, "He is too ashamed of his lies and will probably take good care not to reveal our encounter to anyone." Tomy explained that we are trapped within a society that doesn't allow us to reveal anything which doesn't conform to accepted reasoning. I countered that he was talking about the zeitgeist, a phenomenon that I had been struggling against for years with little success. Tomy nodded silently.

"There is no zeitgeist, really, and yet it exists. You are right: all mankind is a prisoner of this nonexistent zeitgeist. We may be allowed to write or say what we think, but if the time isn't right, it is simply ignored. And should you have the power or motivation to trumpet your knowledge into the world, you will quickly end up on the garbage heap of ridicule. You will be excluded from the society of 'reason.'"

Tomy grinned in agreement. But, seeing as the readers of this unbelievable story can't know what I'm talking about, perhaps a bit more explanation of what I mean by zeitgeist is necessary.

A journalist, for example, is a person who collects facts to reveal them to the public. If the word UFO is currently an emotive subject among the dominant figures in society, then he will not write any positive articles about UFOs. His bosses won't allow it. They need to be "sensible." But what happens when the journalist himself, or herself as the case may be, becomes the chief editor. Of course, he will only make it that far, if he has played the game and remained "sensible." As the editor—and I'm talking about the serious press here—he still could never allow a positive article about UFOs onto the title page. UFOs have no right to exist and anyone who claims they do must *a priori* be an idiot. In the eyes of the "sensible" any UFO sighting must relate to a light aircraft, a kite, a hot-air balloon, reflections, hallucinations, invention, fantasy, swarms of mosquitoes, high-flying weather balloons or even unusually bright planets passing by the Earth at exceptional speed.

The "sensible" mantle themselves in the respectability of science, and even pseudoscience when it suits them; they use the methods of denigration and exclusion and never miss an opportunity to profess their objectivity. This society won't even accept "nonsensible" statements even if they come from people who have made it to a position high up the hierarchical ladder. Just imagine if the Pope or president XY suddenly announced he had spoken with aliens. He would be out of office quicker than you could blink. Aliens? Here? You must have a screw loose, my friend! As *Chariots of the Gods?*—the English edition of my first book—climbed to the top of the U.S. bestseller list in February 1969, many famous and not so famous critics were keen to write their appraisals of my work. So far, so good.

Criticism is an intrinsic part of both science and democracy, but alongside legitimate criticism came barefaced lies, cooked up in the kitchen of disinformation and smuggled into the mass operations of the media. An increasingly negative image developed which was, of course, taken on board by other journalists. The well-known phenomenon: *Catch 22*. Soon it was taboo in "sensible" circles to say anything positive about my books at all. Curiously, my ideas cropped up in all sorts of publications and even TV series—but my name was never mentioned in connection with them. Media and science have let themselves be monopolized; they have lost their innocence and there is no longer anyone left who has the courage to correct the mistake.

Zeitgeist is a collective suppression of those things that we, in our epoch, find too disagreeable to accept. This ominous spirit reminds me of the story of the man whose house was overrun with rats and who assured every visitor: "Rats? There are no rats here, my friend!" and didn't even admit the truth when his children were bitten by the rats and ran around screaming, or when the half-eaten body of the long-missed mother-in-law was found in the cellar. The zeitgeist insists that it is sensible, clever, morally defensible and, of course, all- knowing. But it is killing progress.

Do you understand now, dear reader, what Tomy and I meant by zeitgeist?

As we were eating our lunch on the veranda, Ebet noticed a vintage green Citroën, one of those old cars which had a hood that opened from the side. The car, which bore a French license plate, was parked by the sidewalk, some 100 meters away from the house. Two men sat inside, one of them, armed with a Nikon, was constantly taking photos of our villa. I could recognize the camera, even from a distance, because I had used one myself for years. It was specially developed for sports photographers. The car moved off and took another position around 200 meters further along on the other side of the street. I ran out and tried to stop them from driving away, but the Citroën was quicker than I was.

"So it begins," said Tomy wryly. Ebet suggested that we call the police, but we didn't bother. What would have been the use? I called Marc and asked him if he had told anyone about Tomy. He assured us that he had told no one apart from his mother and his sisters, and he had never mentioned the fact that Tomy was an extraterrestrial. He asked if he should come over to our place for a while, after all we had enough room. I told us we should perhaps wait a while.

Our awakening on the third night at home might have ended badly if it hadn't been for Neptune. He suddenly started barking loudly and the other two dogs quickly joined in. Neptune ran wildly up and down the stairs jumping up at the door handles to every room that was occupied. We ran downstairs, Ebet armed with a flashlight and I with the pistol, which I had grabbed from my nightstand without even thinking about it. Downstairs, Neptune leapt up at the door handle to the veranda, barking ferociously as if he was ready for action. I wasn't sure, but I thought I saw a figure in the darkness loping off across the grass and disappearing into the trees. I opened the door and the dogs shot out. We heard a car engine start, but didn't see any headlights. By the time we caught up with the dogs, they were still barking furiously and were attempting to climb over the garden wall.

Out of breath and extremely agitated, we returned to the veranda. The dogs didn't seem to want to calm down at all. I saw a packet of my cigarettes and a lighter on the rustic table. I was about to light one up, but Tomy grasped my arm.

"Can't you smell it? It stinks of gasoline here!"

I put the lighter back down carefully; Ebet opened the veranda doors wide and the dogs shot back out into the frosty winter's night. Neptune suddenly halted, sniffing at the ground, his long front legs slightly splayed. He trampled around in a circle, investigating something. Where he was standing, just by the wall, where the plants climbed the side of the house almost up to the roof, lay a rag soaked in gasoline. Bravely, I picked up the stinking lump and threw it out onto the garden. Just a single burning match would have been enough to set the entire wall ablaze, right up to the roof.

"They wanted to burn us in our beds!" Ebet stated, steaming with fury. "Now we have to call the police—no matter what you two say!" Then she hugged Neptune and the other two animals in gratitude.

The experts the police sent over were unable to ascertain any more than we could tell them: attempted arson was the verdict. "Have you got any enemies?" asked the oldest of the policeman. Of course, I have. Anyone who writes about subjects that are 'inconvenient' always has.

"I don't mean opponents of your ideas, sir," the arson expert replied. "I mean real enemies who might want to see you dead. To carry out such a base act as this you need to really hate someone quite a lot."

The three officers made notes, packed the gasoline-soaked rag in an evidence bag, looked around for fingerprints, and asked us who was living in the house. We produced Tomy, being careful not to say anything about his origins. Finally, they told us—this was supposed to make us feel better—that they would send regular patrols past our house for the next few days, but we should seriously consider getting an alarm system installed.

It wasn't possible to organize a decent alarm straight away, so I called Marc and my brother Otto and asked them to come over and stay with us for a few days. Our only option was to keep constant watch, around the clock if necessary. Tomy assured us that we needn't fear a second incident: our enemies were warned. Maybe the whole thing had just been an attempt to intimidate us. After all, the other side must have known about the dogs beforehand. Ebet suggested that Tomy and I go up to a hotel in the mountains, but neither of us wanted to leave her on her own.

Otto was two years younger than me—an engineer by trade and an absolute science fiction fan. He accepted Tomy's strange existence immediately as the sober truth. This led to fantastic and highly interesting conversations, which Marc eagerly joined in. Otto asked Tomy the questions that I—from a kind of respect or reverence—hadn't dared. One of the first of them was whether God existed.

"Of course," answered Tomy.

"You have already told us that the beings of your race are some kind of energy forms. Something like God?"

"Of course not! We are nothing but microscopic components of the universe—like you. God spans the entire universe and the constant cycle of creation. God existed for a long time before we arose."

Tomy explained that what mankind thought of as God had always been there and would always be there. In Tomy's world they called it the "great spirit of creation." The big bang, so beloved by our physicists, was just the beginning of one single universe, just one portion of time and space, whereby time only existed for matter and the oscillations that arose from it. I had picked up that concept somewhere during my journey through the universe without really grasping what it meant. I didn't understand it now either.

I asked if it was something only philosophers could understand. Tomy scoffed at this, saying that philosophical thinking looks at Earth as a closed system— something we have never been. Ebet—a product of her catholic upbringing, as was I—insisted on holding onto her Christian view of God. Tomy, blessed as he was with both his own and my entire knowledge, assured her kindly that he had no intention of offending her sensibilities.

"You aren't," she assured him. "I know Erich's views about religion and all that interests me is what you have to add."

The discussion became ever more complex, so I went off and fetched a tape recorder and although I could set it all down here, word for word, I'm not going to go into so much detail. Rather, I will restrict myself to the main direction of Tomy's explanation. After all, it is of great interest to hear what an extraterrestrial thinks of our Christian God.

"From what I have understood from Erich's thoughts and those of the theologian who I recently visited, the first Christian, Jewish and Moslem ideas of God were those of the 'almighty creator,' since creation was—for them—the entire universe. Then, so tell us Christian teachings, this almighty God created plants, animals and then, as the crowning glory of his creation, mankind. It's written down in the Bible: 'And God saw everything that he had made, and, behold, it was very good.' However, later on he regretted the creation of man 'and it grieved him at his heart.' He corrected his mistake and sent the Flood.

You humans considered this to be a result of a divine error, which simply cannot be. The origin of Christianity is the original sin committed by Adam and Eve in Paradise, a guilt that has been handed down through every generation and could only be erased by the sacrifice of God's son himself. This is where you confuse cause and effect. For God, in his eternal wisdom, must have known in advance that the original humans would commit this crime—do you not see the error of your thinking? You have ascribed qualities such as omnipotence and eternal grace to your biblical God, but a God who was almighty and yet looked on idly while all manner of havoc was wreaked throughout the world can hardly be seen as all gracious.

If he was, however, all-gracious and yet unable to hinder the horrific deeds committed throughout history, then this would exclude his almightiness. Both qualities cannot be united—at least as long as your planet is what it is: a hypocritical collection of people who always think they're right. To find explanations for the inexplicable, you humans have proposed yourselves as the solution. In view of the eternal universe, which is constantly being renewed, the question of God does not arise. Creation is simply there. We, and everything around us, are all products of the creation. And here we find the 'great spirit of creation.' Unlike your theology and the beliefs of simple people, this 'great spirit of creation' is not responsible for your suffering, your wars, and your natural catastrophes.

You must go beyond the idea of an anthropomorphized God. The 'great spirit of creation' is not a person; it is the origin of the eternity of the universe."

I didn't understand the last sentence at all, and the others didn't either.

"You took over a senior figure in the Christian church," Elisabeth broke in. "Christians believe in the original sin and redemption through Jesus Christ. Are you saying that they're all lying?"

Tomy, who seemed extremely human during this phase, shook his head.

"You have a word in German that means both yes and no—*jein*, the combination of *ja* and *nein*," he said. "Not either-or. It means that both possibilities are equally valid. The theologian that I took over is a doctor of theology. His intellect tells him that the story of the original sin and the redemption is false, but his faith overpowers his reason. Faith requires no proof. Faith accepts things regardless of reason. Man is false to the point of artlessness and convinces himself that in the kingdom of God the impossible is possible. Believers, inasmuch as they even have the courage for critical analysis, lie to themselves."

Unavoidably, Otto also wanted to know whether there were other beings in the universe like human beings, and Tomy's answer corresponded in many points to what I already knew and had discussed in my books (so I won't repeat it here).

I felt a little flattered that I had been able to filter out a few things over the decades that weren't so far off the mark. The delicate question about time travel also cropped up that afternoon. Otto claimed stiffly that time travel must be impossible because of the dangerous paradoxes it would cause. (You know the story: man travels into the past, meets his own grandfather, and somehow kills him. If this meeting takes place before the man's father is born, then logically the man himself could never be born to travel back in time in the first place. It's the classic paradox.)

That indefinable Mona Lisa smile fluttered across Tomy's lips yet again. It always appeared when he knew something but wasn't quite sure how to put it into words that we would understand.

"Time travel is, nevertheless, possible," he instructed Otto. "Imagine the network of strings on a tennis racket. When the ball hits the strings it causes a dent. Space is warped. Now instead of the tennis ball, take a tiny, but extremely heavy ball that warps the space around it so much that it becomes a ball around your ball. This microscopic but incredibly heavy ball is the time machine. It can leave the space at any point, even in the past. This much has been formulated on the basis of Einstein's General Theory of Relativity.

What is still beyond your grasp is that when the time machine leaves that warped space it emerges in another dimension, because there are an infinite number of dimensions existing simultaneously at any single point. Figuratively speaking: alongside this room where we are having this discussion are trillions of other rooms only fractions of nanometers away from us, filled with people like us, having a discussion like us, but they are all minutely different. You can kill your grandfather in another dimension, because he is not the grandfather from your dimension."

"That's too much for me," sighed Otto in resignation, "I only had one grandfather and I can't murder him ten times."

Tomy's smile was disarming. None of us had the feeling we were being lectured by a self-opinionated schoolmaster, or anything like that. We were like extras on a film set, gawping children who swallow down truths without being able to verify any of it. We believed him because his personality radiated credibility. Tomy dealt with our objections with the gentleness of the Dalai Lama. What did we know?

"About thirty years ago, the Austrian mathematician Kurt Gödel, recognized that Einstein's General Theory of Relativity allowed for traveling through time. But Gödel's time machine was only possible in a rotating universe. But the universe rotates not." Tomy looked out at a sea of silent faces. Although we didn't understand, we nodded in affirmation. Tomy went over and sat next to Otto—on the broad upholstered arm of his chair.

"Do you know who Kurt Gödel was?" "Not a clue," admitted Otto.

"He was born in Brno in 1906, in what was then the Austro-Hungarian Empire. He studied math in Vienna and physics and later wrote a post-doctoral thesis with the somewhat impossible title: *On formally undecidable propositions in the Principia Mathematica and related systems.*"

"Heavens above!" exclaimed Otto holding his hands up in surrender. "None of us understands any of that!"

"Have a little patience," laughed Tomy. "Gödel shook mathematics to its very foundations, although mathematics of all disciplines is so unutterably logical. He formulated an incompleteness theorem for mathematics and revealed that all formal systems cannot be both consistent and complete. Which is true, but I won't burden you with that."

"I didn't understand any of it anyway," I remarked dryly, "I was never kissed by the muse of higher math. Have you got an example down at our level?"

Tomy switched positions, now squatting on the floor cross- legged. He looked compassionately at the people sat around him.

"OK. The mayor of New York wants to fly with his daughter, a friend of his who is a lawyer and the lawyer's wife to Paris. There are only three seats left on the plane, so the whole group gets on board and flies to France. How is that possible?"

Ebet reacted quickest: "Aha, the daughter must sit on her father's lap!"

Tomy laughed. "No, it's much simpler: the daughter is the lawyer's wife!"

"Eureka!" cried Otto, clapping his hands with delight. "Thank heavens we got all this on tape. Now all I have to do is find one of those nice quantum physicist fellows to explain it all to me."

"Why not?" agreed Tomy. "He will take what you can't understand, wrap it in mathematical formulae and at least his colleagues will be able to understand it. In this universe myriads of realities exist right next to each other, spatially, that is. In truth they are all simultaneous. You can get a vague idea of what I mean by considering a hologram. Put infinite numbers of holograms next to each other, on top of each other, under each other, inside each other. They all exist at the same time, but are all slightly different. Your time machine will always take you to a different reality—or a different hologram, if you will."

What could we say? Elisabeth started handing round fruit; Marc blew smoke rings into the air; Otto stared at the pattern of the carpet in front of him. Tomy turned to me, for a last attempt, although he already knew what my memory contained:

"Maybe it's not possible for you to understand it, Erich. Humans are constantly overwhelmed; you suffer from a state of exhaustion brought on by the multitudes of impressions around you. But if you look inside yourself, you remember the 'show' and recognize the holographic universe."

"And what happens to God?"

"The great spirit of creation is the omnipresence of creation itself. If a large, colorful parrot flies towards you, lands on your window sill and starts croaking sentences at you that you can understand, even though you've no idea where the bird came from, what can you assume?"

I didn't need to consider for long.

"That somewhere someone had taught the parrot these sentences," I said.

"And that's exactly how it is with the great spirit of creation!"

THE GREAT CONFUSION

We let three more people in on the secret of Tomy's existence and organized a round-the-clock watch. We set up spotlights in the garden that looked as if they had been put there to illuminate the shrubs. For 24 hours a day vigilant eyes were guarding the property. The dogs were sent out frequently and at random intervals. The Villa Serdang was enclosed by the wall at the front and by a strong fence around the back. The dogs couldn't run away and Neptune would have chased down any unwelcome visitor quickly. For four days and four nights nothing happened, apart from a phone call from Chantal who called from somewhere to announce that she would like to visit us on Sunday evening. That was in five days' time.

In the meantime, Tomy spent every day lying deathly pale on his bed. Every time he returned from his travels he seemed more and more dejected, I tried to talk to him, to cheer him up, but usually he just smiled and begged my understanding when he didn't want to talk. On the second day after Marc and Otto's arrival, he showed us a perfumed letter he'd received from Edith, our housemaid. She wrote that every time she was near him, she had a feeling of wellbeing—a tingling that seized her thoughts and wouldn't let go. Could he help her?

I advised Tomy to write back, but to formulate his answer in such a way that she didn't land in his bed. Tomy answered as always: he could not lie. Nevertheless, he composed a few lines, which he showed to me before sliding them under Edith's door. He told her that she was a bright and charming being—his words—and that he, too, felt warmth for her. But he had no need for physical contact, for his thoughts moved on another plane. This only served to enflame Edith even more and the next morning he found a second letter. Tomy said he would have to tell Edith about his true identity, and I begged him urgently not to. Edith would not be able to understand or cope with the knowledge.

Three times we sat together after dinner and Tomy described his "visits." He had taken over various scientists with diverse specialties—always with their understanding. One scientist after the other had suggested, by means of mental pictures, the name of a colleague. Tomy would then ask if he could call the colleague and ask him if he would be prepared to take part in a scientific experiment. Only one scientist had even entertained the possibility of thought transference, all the rest had simply laughed but taken part in the experiment anyway—if only for fun. The rest had been routine, Tomy assured us, and the amazement on the part of the scientists had been great. He had used a similar modus operandi with the politicians. All in all he had visited thirty-four different people around the world.

"Thirty-four people in the last few days?" I was shocked, "And now they all know me?"

"Yes," said Tomy simply.

In the following weeks I received several anonymous calls and letters. Most of the callers preferred not to reveal their identities at first. They feared for their reputations, their sanity, and were very insecure about the events that had played out within them. Most of the calls began with the same question:

"Hello, am I speaking to Erich von Däniken?"

"Yes, the original."

"I was given your telephone number by a mutual acquaintance and would really like it if we could get to know each other."

"I have many acquaintances, but a personal appointment depends on my agenda. My appointment calendar is fairly full. Who was the acquaintance who gave you my number, then?"

A clearing of a throat. Then: "Hmmm. I can't recall the family name right now, but does the name Tomy mean anything to you?"

"Of course, why didn't you say so sooner? So, when would you like to talk?"

I talked to all of these people—some of them many times—even those who had contacted me by letter. Nobody tried any funny business—it was a small circle of insiders, people who had had the same experience and weren't looking for publicity. One happy side effect: scientists and journalists who had previously pilloried my work, taking neither my books nor me seriously, suddenly changed their tunes and defended my views.

Looking back now, I can see that since Tomy's visit in late fall of 1987 the positions of countless people seems to have changed. Intellectuals started acting tolerantly—favorably even—towards this Erich von Däniken; they influenced their friends and acquaintances, and the same happened in journalistic circles.

I asked Tomy if he had taken over Chantal in the meantime, to find out if she knew who killed Ercan.

Tomy simply said, laconically, "She'll be here on Sunday." He knew nothing new regarding Ercan. People, said Tomy, may be interesting in that respect, but totally dishonest.

"A planet of lies that robs me of any pleasure I might have had in this body."

"Does that apply to me too?"

"You know yourself when you lie," he laughed, "but your lies, too, are unnecessary. Try doing without them for a while!"

***

On Sunday evening I was jogging through the park with the dogs when Neptune suddenly shot off like a streak of lightning towards the veranda door. The door was closed and with its heavy iron door handles it was one of the very few he couldn't open from outside. As far as I knew, Tomy was in the kitchen helping Ebet with the cooking. Then I heard something that could have been a shot, or any one of a dozen other things, and then a shout that sounded like an order being given in a language I didn't understand. Then the slamming of a car door and the squeal of tires.

Tomy! I suddenly had a dreadful thought. Heavy-legged, like in one of those dreams where you are being chased and can't get away, I found myself unable to move. Tomy! I cried out silently, but my knees failed me and I sank to the grass. The next thing that I felt was a wave of wellbeing, calm, and warmth. Tomy was inside me.

"She did it."

"Who?"

"Chantal."

"*What* did she do?"

"She killed my body."

188

"How? For God's sake *how*?

Tomy showed me what had happened, transmitting the pictures directly into my consciousness like a grim newsreel.

"It was some kind of high-voltage device. The doorbell rang and I went to open the door while Elisabeth stayed in the kitchen. Chantal was standing there in a strange-looking, shiny oilskin overall; she suddenly thrust an object with two electrodes against my body. The current was far higher than the normal Taser that American law enforcer's use. The heart muscle of my body went into spasm."

"*Why*? Tell me why! Quick! Go and take over that good-for-nothing bitch and find out why!"

"I can't. She's dead."

Despite Tomy's calming presence, I was finding it extremely difficult to keep my thoughts from running wild. Wobbling slightly, I stood back up. Elisabeth and Otto appeared at the veranda door. They screamed something, but I wasn't listening. I just staggered off towards them.

Tomy didn't need to explain anything. Smoothly, almost indifferently, images popped into my conscious mind—Tomy playing back the events as they had happened. Him standing at the house door, Chantal in her strange protective suit with the pistol-like weapon in her right hand. Then the pain as Tomy's body convulsed and he attempted to stabilize his own heart. The sudden appearance of a dark Cadillac, its rear door thrown open revealing the commandant from Taftan in Iran. He was wearing a dark jacket, black pants, and a white shirt with a blue tie. Then an image of the commandant springing out of the car, barking an order in Arabic and then—without hesitation—shooting Chantal in the back.

Through Tomy's own eyes, which were now beginning to fade, I saw a second man jump out of the Cadillac. He ran around the car, opened the trunk and then the two of them each grabbed one of Chantal's legs. They dragged her lifeless body into the trunk of the car, swung themselves back onto the rear seat and the car roared off. Finally, I experienced how Tomy left his dying body and entered my consciousness.

By now I had reached the veranda door. Neptune shot by Elisabeth and Otto and stood, hackles raised, in a defensive position next to Tomy's now lifeless body. He didn't sniff around the body, didn't lick him. He simply stood legs apart and with a furrowed brow about a meter away. Elisabeth spoke a few calming words to him. The other two dogs also arrived— neither approached Tomy, whose bent body lay on the carpet just inside the door.

Otto quickly explained that he had been upstairs and had heard the doorbell and then a shot, the slamming of the car doors and the squealing of the tires. Elisabeth had heard nothing from the kitchen. Obviously, Tomy had heard the doorbell, but she had only noticed that he had left the room, nothing more.

Using my most commanding tone I interrupted their explanations:

"Be quiet, you two! Tomy is in me. It is only this body," I pointed to the lifeless form on the floor, "that is dead."

But I could have howled, I felt so helpless.

"Hello Elisabeth, hello Otto," said Tomy with my voice. We took ourselves off to the living room and sat down on the sofa. Tomy described for the others what he had already shown me.

During the explanation the doorbell rang again. Otto went to the door, looking through the spyhole before he opened up. It was Marc. His first reaction was shocked horror as he saw Tomy's dead body lying on the floor. But we quickly ushered him through to where we were sitting, where Tomy—in my voice—welcomed him back.

"Tomy," Marc turned to me, "please show me that you're all right."

I felt Tomy flow out of me. Marc suddenly began to giggle, making 'ooh' and 'aah' noises as he had done back in the Intercontinental in Teheran when Tomy had taken him over for the first time. Ebet and Otto stared back and forth between Marc and me.

"That is uncanny! No, fantastic!" cried Otto, slapping his knee. At just that moment Edith walked in, dissolved into a sobbing bundle of misery.

"Yes, Tomy has passed away," I said to her reassuringly and put my arm around her shoulder. "But you know, Edith, we've been expecting this moment for a long time. Tomy was very ill."

The housemaid tore loose and ran up upstairs to her room. Tomy, now speaking through Marc, noted, "You should get rid of my body."

Ebet, however, still had questions:

"Why did Chantal kill you? Her of all people? And why on earth did that Iranian commandant shoot Chantal?"

They were questions that I also was desperate to know the answers to. What was a four-star Iranian general doing here in Switzerland? Especially at the very moment that Chantal stood at our door? I had almost forgotten the general with his white temples, his immaculately combed hair, and black armband of mourning.

Tomy spoke, smiling through Marc's youthful features.

"I intend to find all that out. Chantal's body will give me no answers, but the commandant knows me, I was already in him. I think I'll go give him a call," Marc grinned, "and clear up these last few mysteries."

"Why did they take Chantal's body with them," wondered Otto.

"That, I do not yet know," Tomy smiled and Marc shook his shock of blond hair. "There's a time for everything. You just make sure you get rid of my body, and make sure that there are no traces of Chantal's blood in front of the door." Marc came over to me and put his arm around my shoulders:

"The body in the hallway has still got one surprise in store for you." Marc—that is, Tomy in Marc—smiled, and on Marc's youthful face this smile, that we all knew so well, seemed even more disarming than it ever had on Tomy's own body. He leaned his face over to me, pressing his cheek to mine, as if in a parting gesture, and ran his fingers through my hair with a gentleness that the real Marc would never have managed, and whispered, but loud enough for all to hear:

"I will go into quiescence now. I cannot take the commandant over now anyhow. He will be too agitated, and he will be busy with Chantal's body."

"What do you mean quiescence?" I turned to Marc to question Tomy.

"I had the pleasure of visiting an old Buddhist monk. A man who welcomed me into his consciousness as if he had been expecting me his whole life. He is looking forward immensely to my next visit."

"There was no monk among the people who have contacted me so far," I replied.

Marc removed his arm and stood up and went and sat in an armchair opposite me.

"He won't be contacting you—you will be contacting him!" "But I don't know any Buddhist monks!" I protested.

"You will. At some time in the future."

Marc barked a hearty laugh and then all was quiet. Otto distributed a round of Johnnie Walker Black Label whisky. Even Elisabeth, who doesn't normally touch the stuff, took a small sip.

"So, what are we going to do with Tomy's body?" she asked.

We decided that the best thing to do would be to dig a grave among the trees. We went down into the cellar and found two rusty spades and a hoe. It wasn't easy digging such a large hole between the trees—the earth was a tangle of tree roots. While we men were sweating away at our work, Elisabeth went collecting pine branches and then fetched all the flowers out of every vase in the house. We carried Tomy's body, as he was when he had fallen but covered in a plastic table-cloth. Elisabeth scattered the flowers into the grave and then we men seized hold of the bundle and laid it gently down between the blooms. We didn't register Edith, watching everything from her balcony on the first floor.

It turned out to be the strangest funeral that I have ever attended. The four attendees—Ebet, Marc, Otto and I—stood around the grave after we had filled it in and covered it over with the pine branches. We sank our heads respectfully. No one cried, no one prayed. Marc pulled out his cigarette lighter and waved its flame slowly through the air. I followed suit. Elisabeth, inappropriately as ever, sang the first verse of the Beresina-Lied:

> Unser Leben gleicht der Reise
> Eines Wandrers in der Nacht;
> Jeder hat in seinem Gleise
> Etwas, das ihm Kummer macht
>
> (Our life is like a journey
> Of a wanderer through the night;
> Everybody carries something on his way
> That causes him to grieve.)

Otto left us for a moment and returned presently, armed with a whisky bottle, glasses and four candles. We placed the flaming candles between the pine branches, said a toast to Tomy, and then tipped the rest of the bottle on the grave. At some point Elisabeth said that Tomy had been a unique person, she had really liked him. Then she looked at me and fell into my arms. We fought back the tears together.

When a light rain began to fall, Otto inquired, "Who fancies another whisky?"

We trotted back into the house; all of us crestfallen, downbeat but not truly sad. Otto opened another bottle; Elisabeth went off into the kitchen to prepare dinner. Marc, a whisky tumbler in his hand, strolled off to the front door.

"There's blood down there on the path," he noted.

I went and fished a bucket out of the cupboard where we kept the cleaning materials, filled it with water, and sluiced away what was left of Chantal's blood. The fine rain did the rest. We called to Edith, so she could set the table and realized that she must have left the house. Elisabeth guessed that she had gone to her girlfriend's house nearby.

That night was a long one. We discussed many things and shared our memories of Tomy. In the early hours—sometime around seven o'clock, since at this time of year it is still dark—the doorbell rang. Elisabeth went and answered it in her dressing gown. She escorted three policemen into the house and then came and woke us.

"We had a call," began the senior officer, who was in plain clothes, "that a young man had been murdered here."

I feigned innocence; the others said nothing at all. "How on earth did you come by such an idea, officer?"

"Your housemaid, Edith, was at the station house.

Her statement was unambiguous. Would it be all right if we looked around?"

I had a sense of foreboding. But Edith didn't know anything about Tomy's grave—or so I thought. So I told the police officers that Edith was a lovely girl and had probably fallen in love with my younger brother, but he had left the country the previous night.

The plain-clothes man gave me a severe look and shook his head slightly with a what-kind-of-fools-do-you-take-us-for? expression on his face. The officers searched the villa from cellar to attic. One of them discovered Tomy's passport lying on a chest of drawers. The plain-clothes man flicked through it. He put it in his pocket finally and promised us—ominously—that we would be hearing from him.

"Crap!" swore Otto.

Elisabeth said we should have followed Tomy's advice and not lied.

It was obvious to me that it wouldn't take the authorities long to find out that the passport wasn't kosher. No Anton von Däniken had ever been born on April 24, 1954, in Zofingen. What was I to do? How was I to explain Tomy's existence and disappearance to the Swiss detectives? I knew from my late brother-in-law that they were well trained, highly capable and stubborn, and thorough and patient into the bargain. Elisabeth was all for telling everything. We should show the police Tomy's grave. After all, we were all witnesses to what had really happened. But, as usual, things didn't turn out as expected.

We hadn't quite finished breakfast and I was still slurping my morning tea when two police cars pulled up. Six men armed with shovels and pickaxes got out, preceded by Edith who led them directly to the spot in the trees where Tomy's body lay.

"This is where it is," she said with a pinched

smile. The triumph in her voice was unmistakable. I could have strangled her.

Despite the drizzling rain, the traces of candle wax from the night before were still plain enough. It wasn't particularly difficult for the police diggers to remove the loose earth from the grave and in no time at all they were almost done. I was ready to confess everything, but didn't want to do it in front of all these men. Then one of them men struck pay dirt. They all jumped in and swiped aside the remaining earth with their hands. They revealed Tomy's black shoes and socks, his dark blue pants and the blue-red striped shirt. All of it soaking wet as if it had just been pulled out of a bath. Where did all this water come from? It couldn't have come from the rain. That would have all drained straight through into the ground below. I expected to see Tomy's mud-streaked hair at any second, but there was no head, no hands, and no legs, either. Nothing at all. The sopping wet clothes were simply empty. As was the plastic tablecloth that we used to lower Tomy into the grave, which still—I was convinced—smelled of whisky with a touch of magnesium. No body, not a single hair. Just water and a highly strange aroma.

The officers stood up, brushing the dirt from their hands. "What's all this about?" asked the chief with the serious face.

"I told you that there wasn't anybody here," I countered, not knowing if I should laugh or cry. The policeman ordered his men to dig deeper, but there was nothing to find.

The chief turned again to me, a grim look on his face.

"So tell me, why did you hold a candlelit burial for a bunch of soaking wet clothes?" he asked.

"Have you never heard of a cenotaph? It's an unfilled grave, like they had in ancient Greece and Egypt. An empty monument to a departed friend, so to speak."

"So where's the real grave?"

"There isn't one, because nobody is dead. We celebrated my younger brother's departure last night."

"You think you're so very clever, Mr. von Däniken" said the detective contemptuously, adding a "tsk, tsk." "We will be initiating proceedings against you and your companions. No one is to leave the house. And you—Mr. von Däniken—are coming with me."

In the station house in Solothurn the questioning began. I insisted that an examining magistrate be called in from the very beginning. He arrived a half an hour later, rather grumpily, it seemed to me.

"So, Mr. von Däniken," he said, in an attempt at civility, "you are a clever man and have written lots of books. So make it easier on yourself and for us. Every lie you tell us just draws out the time you spend in custody."

"Am I under arrest then?"

"That can be arranged with a simple signature. So come on, don't beat around the bush!"

I could have demanded a lawyer, but he would have been just has perplexed as the examining magistrate. So I requested that the clerk, who was writing everything down for the file, be sent out of the room.

I said that they could leave the tape recorder running and I would tell them everything: the truth, the whole truth and nothing but the truth. And then sign the statement without any protest. And that was exactly what happened.

I spoke from 8 a.m. till around three in the afternoon. Only stopping to drink mineral water and eat a sandwich. The magistrate had grinned, hammered his fists on the table, changed the cassettes, prowled round the room and repeatedly asked me if I was completely normal, stating that he was convinced that someone like me should be in a psychiatric clinic.

"Mr. Kellerhans," as the examining magistrate was called, "we could make all this a lot shorter if you were to interview Marc and my wife. If they tell the same story, then we must all be crazy!"

"You could have all got your stories straight beforehand," said Kellerhans unimpressed. "But we'll get you, don't worry. So let's start again—from the beginning."

He left the room for a moment, gave some orders, and returned with an unidentifiable grin on his face. I started telling my story again from the beginning. After an hour or so, he stopped me and decided to take a break. He ordered me not to leave the room. But at least he had some tea sent in.

He didn't return until two hours and 18 cigarettes later. This time he had Elisabeth, Marc, and Otto with him.

"I could have all four of you arrested," he announced arrogantly and then shifted nervously from one foot to the other. "But as yet, we have a murder with no body. Your statements could have all been worked out together. We will check every single detail." He looked sternly at me: "Bearing in mind your standing, your fixed residence here and the particular circumstances of this case, and under advice of the state prosecutor, I am going to let you go home—for the time being. On the condition, Mr. von Däniken, that you and the other three remain in Solothurn. Any contravention of this and I will order your immediate arrest!"

I thanked him insincerely, but was immensely relieved to have gotten out of this tricky situation, at least for now.

In the following days specialists from the forensic unit and the police's scientific department went through the villa and grounds with a fine-tooth comb. They didn't just turn Tomy's room inside out, they checked out every armchair that he'd ever sat in. Any object he'd ever touched was confiscated, especially all his clothes, even underwear. Again and again I had to trudge into town, to the police station, often accompanied by Marc, Otto and Elisabeth.

We were always interrogated separately. I lost count of the amount of times that I was asked the same questions. But the faces didn't remain the same: psychologists, secret service agents, scientists all turned up. Their expressions always became increasingly serious, more confused, and sometimes even angry. Finally, after a break of five days in a row without having a single summons, I humbly asked the examining magistrate if he would allow me to travel to St. Moritz and spend a week in the Suvretta House Hotel. I really needed a break.

"There are conditions," he warned sternly, "You are not to leave St. Moritz. You are to report in every day by telephone and you are to speak to no one—I repeat, no one!—about this affair." We were given an explicit order to treat the case as "secret."

So it was, at the beginning of December in the year 1987 that I traveled to the winter wonderland of Engadin. Before I invited Marc to join me, I asked the examining magistrate if it would be OK. He had no objection.

"But only him!" he warned me. "Apart from him, you are to talk to no one. Is that understood?"

A CHRISTMAS MIRACLE

Marc and I are now back home. I managed to type 263 pages of this report into my computer while I was at the Suvretta House. On the very first day after our return Mr. Kellerhans, the examining magistrate, summoned me to his office. This time he was much friendlier than he had been at the earlier interviews. The scientists had discovered exonerating evidence; the Swiss secret service had contacted their colleagues in Iran. Because Switzerland had excellent diplomatic relations with Iran and what's more were representing the U.S.A. in the country many things seemed possible that I would not have believed before.

"From the very first day that we interviewed you, we started trying to locate Mr. Shubika…"

"Who on earth is that?" I interrupted him.

"The four-star general from the barracks in Taftan. It is not acceptable for foreign agents to be active in the territory of the Swiss Confederation. Let alone commit murder."

"So you believe me now?"

Kellerhans turned to me: "Belief is the domain of religion. I believe nothing. But I and several of our experts do not preclude the possibility that your version of events is true."

"And? Have you found the general? And how does that help you?"

The examining magistrate rocked in his chair, spread his fingers, and laid his hands on his desk. Tilting his head slightly, he said:

"The general was taken over by Tomy in Taftan, so you said. That means, he can confirm Tomy's existence. What's more, he killed Chantal. Why?" Kellerhans leaned forward and raised a finger: "He is the key to this case."

He looked at me with an uncharacteristically friendly expression on his face. "Anyway, we still haven't found Ms. Babey's body. And neither have the French."

Again sworn to secrecy, I was told that the Swiss secret service had gotten involved and had been in contact with some of their highest-ranking counterparts in both France and Iran. In both cases, the circle of those in the know was kept extremely small—the case could not be allowed to become public. An incident such as this was not only one for the astronomers who have been searching in vain for extraterrestrial life for decades, but could throw the general public into panic. I should just think about it, he said, and I would know he was right.

"Has Tomy contacted you again since his…erm …departure?"

"No," I answered truthfully. "To be honest, I am expecting him at any moment."

"When he … erm … arrives, could you perhaps ask him if he would take me over?"

"*You?*" I stared at Kellerhans slack-jawed.

"Just think about it, Mr. von Däniken," he said. "If Tomy can take *me* over then *you* are completely off the hook. Do you understand? Then I will close your file and bury it."

I scratched my chin. Tomy should take over the examining magistrate? For the time being, I didn't have any idea where

Tomy was. Since that evening when he had taken his leave of us, telling us that he was returning to his quiescent state in a Buddhist monk, we hadn't heard a peep. So I promised Mr. Kellerhans that I would pass on his request as soon as Tomy made contact. I still had one question for him, though. How long was he expecting to keep this case under wraps?

"That's not for me to decide," he replied. "But the usual period of time for cases like this is twenty years."

Nineteen years have now passed since that day. One year more or less can hardly matter now. I have decided, regardless of my obligations, to tell the whole story. Even if it is only in the form of a novel.

***

It had gotten cold outside. Even the lowlands—Solothurn was only a few hundred meters above sea level—were covered in snow. A roaring fire burnt every night in the hearth of the Villa Serdang on the road from Feldbrunnen on the outskirts of Solothurn. Every now and again Marc turned up for dinner. The housemaid, Edith, had long since handed in her notice. She couldn't live under the same roof as murderers, she wrote in her resignation letter. The examining magistrate gave me permission to leave my property and move freely around Switzerland. I hardly went to my office at all, only dealing with those things I absolutely had to. I read a lot of newspapers, or went Christmas shopping with Elisabeth. We had told my sister Leni all about Tomy's demise and hammered into her that some high state office had ordered that the whole affair remain secret. But inside, I remained churned up and agitated. Why didn't Tomy get in contact? What could have happened to him?

Christmas Eve went off as it always did. Leni and Elisabeth cooked various vegetables, made salads and desserts: I was responsible for the deliciously browned turkey. Our entire extended family, including brothers- and sisters-in-law and associated children feasted merrily around a large oval table. Candles flickered, reflecting in the glasses, and the scent of pine needles drifted pleasantly through the house. Presents, laughter and thank-you kisses and hugs were the order of the night. In the background, Christmas music played softly over the speakers of the stereo.

Toward the end of the party, I suddenly felt a gentle wave roll through my consciousness, almost as if a radio station had gotten mixed up with my thoughts. And then came a telepathic giggle.

"Yes, that's about right!"

Despite all my experiences with Tomy, I began laughing loudly from relief. Especially as he had arrived just as the carol "From heaven on high, I come to you" was playing.

"Indeed, Tomy! Your arrival is just like a visit from an angel coming down from heaven!"

"Happy Christmas!" he replied. "Can you spare me a moment or two?"

I quickly told everyone about Tomy's arrival. The adults already knew about him, and only the children asked curiously who Tomy was. I explained that he was my best friend, and I certainly didn't feel that that was a lie. I strolled upstairs in a leisurely fashion, grinning constantly, and lay down on my bed. The answers that Tomy gave me now didn't come via my thoughts. In some wonderful way I saw, felt, and heard everything he had to tell me.

The first series of images Tomy showed me featured the commandant of the Taftan barracks. As Tomy softly slipped into his consciousness, he was reading a newspaper. He was sitting at a desk in a large room in his parent's house. In civilian clothing. He was not surprised by Tomy's visit—he had been expecting him.

"I knew you would come," he murmured out loud. "I've been expecting you since I got home. I'm no longer in the army, you know. I'm a civilian now. You'll be wanting to know why I shot Chantal. Well, it was because she killed my beloved son. In a cruel and agonizing manner." A surge of bitterness flowed through his consciousness.

That made everything more complicated. Up till now I hadn't known anything about a son. He hadn't appeared over the last few months. And Chantal was supposed to have killed this lad in an agonizing way?

Gently, as if he didn't want to overload my brain, Tomy played back the events before my mind's eye.

The commandant had only had one son, Chalid, and two daughters. I could see the lad as if he was standing before me. He was tall and slim with soft hands and fingers that could have belonged to a pianist. Raven-black hair and the beginning of a beard framed his tanned face. His carefree laughter revealed ivory-white teeth. And then Chantal entered the picture. She didn't look much different than the way she had when we had known her, and she used her striking looks and her irresistible feminine charms to worm her way into Chalid's affections. He didn't stand a chance. The commandant—I'll stick with this appellation now—did not approve of the liaison between his son and Chantal. True, he did not begrudge his son this amorous adventure, such a thing is a matter of course in the Arab world, but the age difference between the two worried him.

He would have preferred to see Chalid matched with a girl from a good Iranian family. The commandant had always imagined that his son would start a career in the civil service and enter politics, but instead the lad decided to study medicine. He had already completed one and half semesters at the university in Teheran. Chantal somehow managed to convince the commandant's family that Chalid would be better off in Paris, where the possibilities for specialist training were much better than in Iran. Chalid transferred to Paris and moved into an apartment with Chantal. This was the summer of 1986.

In the following months Chalid visited Iran several times; every time looking more worn down and unhealthy. The doctors in Iran diagnosed leukemia, but the less aggressive form that could be kept in check with medication. Chalid set his hopes on scientific research someday finding a drug that would cure him completely. During one short visit to Teheran Chalid confessed to his sister that Chantal was cheating on him. She was rarely in their shared apartment; he had even hired a private eye to follow her. She had turned into a regular whore who had nothing but sex in mind, and she was abusing him terribly. They had had fierce rows, but nothing had changed.

Only two weeks before Marc, Tomy, and I had turned up in the barracks where the commandant was stationed, Chalid had died in a Teheran hospital. The family was suffering terribly; their grief was unbearable. That was the reason he had been wearing the black armband.

The commandant, who had been talking out loud

the whole time even though Tomy would have under-stood him anyway, laid his arms on the desk. Images of the meal we had taken together in the Sahedan Inn hotel in Zahedan appeared—I remembered the smoked salmon and "Omar Sharif." After this meal Chantal had handed over a letter that contained financial de-mands. She bemoaned her fate since Chalid's death, both in terms of her heartbreak and how he had left her without a penny. A few days later his eldest daughter had told him the truth about Chantal's infidelity, her sexual appetite, her whoring around and how she had humiliated Chalid. These revelations and Chantal's demands for money had raised his suspicions. He had contacted an old friend in the secret service and had arranged to have Chalid's body exhumed.

"Do you know why my beloved son Chalid got leukemia?" he asked in a loud and furious voice and then said to Tomy in his thoughts, "Yes, my friend Tomy, you know. This disgusting woman poisoned my son with some kind of radioactive material. She must have been doing it for months while Chalid was wasting away in agony. He suffered so terribly, and all the time she was treating him like dirt. She deserved a slow and painful death, but I shot her!"

The commandant laid his head in his hands and wept. A brigadier general, who had probably killed many people in his early career, and now a broken man.

Tomy followed the traces of his memory, wanting to know why the commandant was there at the *Villa Serdang* at precisely the moment that Chantal had car-ried out her murderous deed. The commandant stood up and paced around the room.

He spoke loudly, as if he were talking to someone in the room with him.

"It is good indeed, my friend—for I see you as a friend, because you are not of this terrible world—to be able to talk to you," he said. "You know that I myself was an active agent in SAVAK, the Shah's secret police. It was not a happy time. We did much that I am not proud of, and I have regretted my deeds ever since. If there is forgiveness in another world, then I ask Allah to forgive me. May he have mercy on my soul. My family helped many of the victims from back then. They didn't even know where the help came from.

I was a high-ranking officer in SAVAK; my family was one of the wealthiest in the land; my grandfather had an oil well on his own land. After the regime changed I ran a training camp here in Teheran; later they packed me off to Taftan. But I kept some of my old contacts intact. Without these contacts I would never have been able to exhume Chalid—Allah have mercy on him. It was comrades from back then who identified the radiation damage in his bones."

Still lying on my bed, I slowly began to see connections, the existence of which I had never even suspected before.

Everything that the commandant spoke out loud, I experienced through Tomy's consciousness in sound, picture, and all the senses. I felt the touch of a breeze, smelled—without a nose and without being there—the stale aroma of old cigars. I saw, if you could call it seeing, the commandant as a secret service man, as a colonel in the training camp, felt his pain as much as his need for reparation and redemption. I experienced his bitterness, about himself and the world. Whenever the commandant opened a window, walked around the room, sat down or anything else, Tomy was with him. And so was I, so I felt. He talked to Tomy's consciousness as though he were talking to someone in the room, sitting opposite him.

"You want to know the details? I will tell you everything! Tomy, I would be so grateful if you could take me with you when you return to your world. Yes, I understand that it's not possible. But could you put in a good word for me? Is forgiveness possible?"

I could feel Tomy's answers. He soothed the commandant, showed him glimpses of his home world, and explained the divinity of creation, the "great spirit of creation."

"So, there will be forgiveness, if I want it and make good my errors. That helps me a lot, thank you."

He paused a moment, and then continued:

"I found out from my friends, one of whom—you can see him in my mind—is the head of the secret police, about the plans to eliminate you. You, my dear friend, were ranked as the single most dangerous being alive. You were to be removed from this world, radically and for good. And your friends, too, although they weren't considered quite so dangerous, of course. They tried to arrange to have you all killed in an accident on Mount Nemrut in Turkey. There was a great deal of anxiety when you all emerged unscathed. Somebody suggested using a fast-working poison gas to do the job, but the attendant circumstances for innocent bystanders were too unpredictable.

The physicist—a top man in the service—pointed out to the committee that it was impossible to just kill you because your consciousness would simply spring to another body. They had seen that demonstrated clearly enough in Teheran. Tomy, you know that I am telling the truth—no, think!—I was against it. But as a nonmember of the service, my influence was limited. The conversations I had with my ex- colleagues didn't take place on government property, but in a coffee house. That was where I found out about their perfidious plans to put you out of action. The physicist recommended a massive electric current that would have to be applied—so he believed—to your body at lightning speed and with the element of surprise. Your consciousness would be shocked, taken by surprise and you would not have time to leave your body. Allah be praised that you survived the attack!" He was silent for a moment and then: "Did you suffer?"

"No," Tomy's consciousness answered kindly. "I was surprised for a second by Chantal's grim expression. She stood there on the doorstep baring her teeth like a dog. I wanted to speak to her, but I never had a chance. She must have hit me with around 50,000 volts. I didn't feel any pain, and my first priority was to try and stabilize the heartbeat in my body. I caught a glance of your Cadillac, commander, but didn't hear the shot that you fired. I saw how Chantal's mouth fell open in shock; how she didn't understand what was happening to her; how her eyes rolled up and she fell to one side. The last thing I saw with Tomy's eyes was a second man who was helping you to drag Chantal's body to the open trunk of the car. Then I sprang into Erich."

"Ah yes, the writer." The commandant conjured up a tired smile: "How is he? Say hello to him from me and tell him it'll soon all be over."

Again Tomy had to calm the commandant's troubled thoughts. He regained a measure of control and managed to light up a fresh cigar.

"How did you know exactly when Chantal was planning to attack?" asked Tomy.

The commandant seemed relieved. The strange exchange of thoughts between his consciousness and Tomy's "intelligent energy," but also the understanding that Tomy signalized and the generosity, with which he accepted the commandant's confession, soothed his nerves greatly.

"During my time with SAVAK, I never heard anything about electroshock weapons. They weren't around then. My friend, the head of the secret police, told me all about them one afternoon in the coffee house, and all about the planned assassination on that Sunday evening in Switzerland. Chantal was given the shocker in Paris. Please, no—you know it, my alien friend—not this tramp, of all people. Not the whore who killed my beloved son in such an insidious manner. *She* was to kill you. I was *against* your murder, Tomy!"

The commandant managed a liberating laugh: "It was only a few days after I had found out for sure about the true causes of Chalid's death. And now, the order for your elimination, Tomy. It was simply too much. My plan was to get to your friend Erich's villa *before* Chantal arrived. I even called on the phone, to warn you. But nobody answered the phone. As I saw the whore standing in the doorway in front of your body, I was hoping against hope that she hadn't discharged the weapon yet. I cried out, as loud as I could 'Desist immediately!' but even from behind I could see her right arm crooked and I shot her immediately in the back. Allah knows that is not my way. But I had to react with lightning speed, Tomy. I wanted to save you. If Chantal hadn't had the electro-shocker in her hand and aimed at your body, we could have overpowered her and taken her back to Iran to face the courts."

He wiped his sweating brow with an oversized handkerchief, puffed on his cigar and asked, prepared deep down to reveal even his most intimate of secrets, if there was anything else Tomy still wanted to know.

"What happened to Chantal's body?" Tomy asked.

We drove her in the Cadillac to a farm in the Jura Mountains. The Swiss friend of mine has a farm there. We hacked the body into tiny pieces and threw the whole lot—clothes and all—into a large vat of hydrochloric acid. There wasn't a trace left."

Still lying on my bed in the Villa Serdang, I let out a large sigh. Tomy's revelations filled me with increasing astonishment. There wasn't the slightest doubt that the commandant was telling the truth: Tomy had experienced everything via his consciousness— and I had the privilege of being present in Tomy's incredible vibrations. As I looked up, I saw Elisabeth gazing down at me from the foot end of the bed. I could hear the laughing of children from down below. Just like the first time in Ankara, this "journey" had only taken a few seconds. Elisabeth must have followed me up here the moment I left the table.

"What's the news?" she asked.

"I know the basics," I answered, still a little bewildered. "It's an unbelievable story! There are still a few things I'd like to find out though ..."

"...Greetings Elisabeth ..." Tomy broke in using my voice. " Allow me just a few more minutes with your wonderful husband; he'll be back down at the party in a short while."

Alone again, I asked Tomy: "And what about Ercan? Why did he have to go?"

Tomy played back the next part in small fragments inside my head. It was the same scene as before: still in the commandant's house in Teheran. The room stank even more intensely of stale cigar smoke than before. Strange. I lay on my bed, in my own bedroom in my own house, and could smell the acrid aroma of cigars from a room thousands of kilometers away. And what made it even crazier: this meeting had taken place weeks before I experienced the rerun on Christmas Eve, 1987. I gave up trying to think about what kind of ethereal pathways were necessary to make all this possible and held on to Tomy's idea of the "holographic universe."

In faraway Teheran—all those weeks ago—the

commandant opened a window and threw the butt of his cigar into a gravel- filled container that was standing below. After taking a few deep breaths, he returned to the desk where he had been sitting a few minutes earlier.

"Yes, the episode with Ercan Güsteri," he murmured aloud, seemingly talking to himself. "I didn't find out about it until Mr. Güsteri was already dead. A sickening affair, for which Chantal—indirectly, at least—was again responsible, even though she wasn't actually directly involved in his murder."

"This Ercan and the whore Chantal," he added a curse in Arabic, "had intimate contact with each other. Chantal told her new lover everything she knew about you, every single tiny detail. She told him of the events in the Intercontinental Hotel in Teheran and about how you had helped in the search for terrorists. She told him how she had been there while you had taken over the consciousnesses of other people, including an ayatollah and a wealthy oil merchant. She even told him about the experiment with the physicist. Ercan Güsteri—may Allah have mercy on his soul—didn't believe a word about your 'extraterrestrial energy,' my dear friend, but he was convinced of the existence of certain parapsychological abilities, including psi factors. You have to realize, Tomy, that Ercan was a high-ranking member in an extreme right-wing Turkish organization. Well, anyway, there are informers everywhere, and thanks to one of ours we found out that they were planning to kidnap you, Tomy. They honestly believed that they could incapacitate you somehow and keep you captive. Not because you were an extraterrestrial, of course—nobody believed that story—but because of your abilities. Their aim was to make you compliant and use your talent to achieve their political aims by taking over certain politicians and turning them. Those idiots in Ankara didn't realize that trying to hold you captive was pointless: it didn't even occur to them that all you would have to do was jump into one of their leaders and turn *him* …"

Tomy smiled. "True indeed," he conveyed to the commandant's mind. "My earthly body, that of Tomy, was certainly mortal enough, Chantal proved that. And if these people had tried to inflict pain on me I could have taken over the torturer in a nanosecond. I would have brought the whole group to their knees—from the torturer to the head of the group."

Now the commandant laughed: a liberating experience. "You are good! Someone like you should be a friend for life!"

"My time here is almost over," Tomy told him soberly. "Back home, everyone will be desperate to hear about all my news and experiences on this planet of lies." He quickly changed the subject back to Ercan: "Couldn't the Iranian secret police have used some other method to make Ercan see sense? Did he have to die because of what he knew?"

"It was the committee's decision. Ercan was one of a group of fanatics who weren't particularly receptive to reason. In Teheran they wanted to make sure that you, my dear friend Tomy, were dead, and that your … erm, your energy form wasn't floating around somewhere out there. For that reason, as you already know, they decided on the plan with the electroshock weapon. If Ercan's group had gained control of your physical body, we would never have been sure that you wouldn't turn up here again sometime, wanting your revenge… not a nice thought, especially now that I know more about your capabilities."

"Revenge" Tomy thought, "is something we do not know."

I had dimmed the light in my room. Now I blinked

into the weak light of the lamp and spoke to Tomy's consciousness:

"What a God-awful planet!"

Tomy managed a giggle, a form of expression he had learnt while here. He seemed to enjoy doing it.

"There's nothing wrong with the planet. It's fantastic. The human race is awful. But I have had the opportunity to meet some wonderful people."

That was a comfort. He went on to tell me that the Iranians had wanted to deal with us while we were still in Turkey, but somehow they had managed to lose track of us. The trick with the fake airline bookings and the *Orient Express* had worked! Hurrah! I asked Tomy how long he was going to stay around. A couple of days, he explained, and then he was going to visit his friend, the Buddhist monk, one more time.

"Will you say goodbye before you go?" I wanted to know.

"Of course, my friend."

I felt Tomy begin to pull away and then suddenly remembered: "Stop Tomy, stop!" I cried mentally. "The examining magistrate, Mr. Kellerhans, he wants you to take him over. Then all my troubles will be over." A thought suddenly struck me: "Which reminds me: why didn't the police find your body?"

Again he giggled: "You can tell the examining magistrate I'd be happy to drop by. And my body? That body was put together in an extremely short time, not in a natural way either. When my energy, the vibrations that were keeping the molecules together, was removed from the body, the disintegration process began. Within three hours, all the elements that had been taken to construct my body had been given back to the earth."

And then Tomy left. I didn't wait around; I went straight back down to my family. The candles around the Christmas tree were burnt down now. I uncorked a bottle of rosé champagne and said to the adults that I would tell them everything, but not until the children had gone to bed. Then I called Marc. His festive celebrations were also already over so he put himself in a taxi and drove over to join us.

It was already midnight, by the time everyone was gathered again around the table, this time filled with anticipation.

"I have an unbelievable tale to tell you all..."

WHAT HAPPENED NEXT?

January 1, 1988, was the last time I ever heard from
Tomy. I was strolling around the meadow behind the
Villa Serdang, taking deep refreshing breaths of the
cold, crisp winter air and breathing out the residual
alcohol from our New Year's Eve celebrations, when I
suddenly perceived Tomy's giggle inside my head.

"Happy New Year! And while I'm thinking about
it, may all your coming years be happy and successful,
too! May you stay healthy and write even better than
ever before!"

"Tomy!" I now talked to him as if he was a physical presence. "It's great to see you again!"

"You don't need to tell me! I can feel it! Quickly,
Erich, bring us both to a room, where we can have a
few minutes undisturbed."

On the way to my library, Tomy told me that he
had taken over Kellerhans. He was now a happy man
and had even gone out and bought some of my books.
He had visited others too: the chief of the Iranian secret police, and even the state president. He had convinced them that Tomy no longer existed and that

there was nothing to fear from the remaining participants in this strange story. All of the activities aimed
toward us had been called off.

I sat down in the swivel chair in the library.

"I presume you have come to say goodbye. Is
there anything

I can do to convince you to stay?"

I suddenly had a feeling as if I was being stroked
gently, although I was completely alone in the room.

"I feel something that I suppose you would call
homesickness. And anyway, I know enough about the
human race, your history and your systems. But before
I go, I want to give you a present, Erich."

What happened next was simply indescribable. I
raced away from the Earth and into the universe, saw
even more incredible images than I had the first time
during my fantastic journey in the Sheraton Hotel in
Ankara, and then, suddenly, I was laying on a green
meadow, even though my body was sitting on a swivel
chair in my library. Tomy appeared before me as a
beautifully shimmering light. This light bored into my
soul and I heard a voice, though I had no ears: "The
entire knowledge of this planet is stored in the electrons. Add a little energy to the atoms and the electrons will spring from one atom to the next. You
subconscious can tap this knowledge in this way. You
only need to be peaceful and calm. Look into yourself
and the information will simply flow into your consciousness."

My eyes flashed open and I found myself sitting
back in my library.

"Tomy, wait! Thank you, thank you! I think I understand how it works. Will you come again?"

"That is not possible!"

"Why not?" I wanted to know.

"Because this planet is merely an infinitesimal part

of a myriad of solar systems and I would never be able to find it again. Think about the holographic universe. And make contact with the Buddhist monk!"

And then something happened that even the best writer in the world—and I'm a long way off being that—wouldn't have been able to describe. A kind of collection of "soft filaments," which were spewing out endorphins, caressed my consciousness. Tiny sparks of light, which tasted like the buds of wonderfully aromatic blooms, shot through the convolutions of my brain. This must have been the scent of heaven. Any attempt at description is doomed to failure, so I won't even try. What can you compare a smell to when there is no material in existence that is comparable? Tomy had taken his leave.

That same evening I wrote a letter to the monk, who lived in the Buddhist monastery in Ladakh in the highlands of "Little Tibet." Six months later I took an airplane to Srinagar; from there I traveled by car to Ladakh. The meeting I had there with the monk is beyond my ability to describe. We simply held hands, even though this was not really necessary. Each one of we somehow knew everything about eachother.

The next ten books I wrote—between 1988 and 2006—seemed to just flow from my pen. Even *Der jüngste Tag hat längst begonnen* (*Judgment Day is Already Upon Us*), a book that was packed with references, took me only three weeks to write. And I was only writing for four hours a night! I suddenly started receiving invitations to lecture to societies where I would never have dreamed of having the chance to speak before Tomy's visit. The German TV channel Sat.1 commissioned me to create a 25-show series for which I not only wrote the scripts but which I also presented. Then I was invited to the U.S.A. by the *Discovery Channel* to make two TV series. Before I knew what was happening, the British TV company—20/20—did a biography of me, in which I made no mention of Tomy. Subsequently, the international press began treating this controversial author—Erich von Däniken—with much more understanding than they ever had before. I started getting invitations from various scientific circles and universities and even—completely out of the blue—received awards. Finally, I came up with the idea of setting up a park in Interlaken in Switzerland where all the great mysteries of the world would be collected together. I wrote explanatory texts for all of the exhibits and the shows in the pavilions.

And one more thing: I founded the "Non-Liar's Club." Anyone who promises never to lie may join. The youngest member is just 17, the oldest is 87 years old. Many of the club members know each other and no one ever lies. It is an uncomplicated organization with no need for a written charter—just one of the many wonderful ideas that Tomy inspired.

About the Author

Erich von Däniken's first book, *Chariots of the Gods*, became a worldwide bestseller following its publication in 1968 and has been translated into thirty-two languages. It has since been followed by over two dozen additional books, including *The Eyes of the Sphinx*, *Odyssey of the Gods*, and *The Gods Were Astronauts*. Born and educated in Switzerland, Erich is an active researcher and explorer. His books have given rise to two full-length documentary films, *Chariots of the Gods* and *Messages of the Gods*, and he has delivered over 3,000 lectures in twenty-five countries. He lives in Beatenberg, Switzerland, with his wife. *Tomy and the Planet of Lies* is his first work of fiction.